A MOTHER'S PRAYER

CHRIS MADAY SCHMIDT

Recycling programs
for this product may
not exist in your area.

ISBN-13: 978-1-335-62172-6

A Mother's Prayer

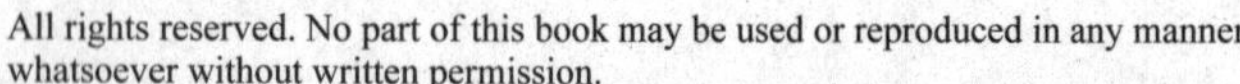

Love Inspired
22 Adelaide St. West, 41st Floor
Toronto, Ontario M5H 4E3, Canada
www.LoveInspired.com

HarperCollins Publishers
Macken House, 39/40 Mayor Street Upper,
Dublin 1, D01 C9W8, Ireland
www.HarperCollins.com

Printed in Lithuania

1 2 3 4 5 6 7 8 9 10 LIT 28 27 26 25

"Something funny you care to share, mister?"

Hank clamped his mouth closed. "No, ma'am."

Olive flicked her wrist toward the door to the garage floor. "Okay then, what's first on the agenda—boss?"

"Pull up a chair." Hank indicated a tall chair with wheels in front of the computer. And for the next hour, he gave her an overview of the accounting software, then disappeared into the shop.

"When will you let me work back there?" she asked, sharper than she meant. But she didn't take it back—she wasn't here to be humored.

"Once everything is caught up—" he waved an arm at the mess on the workspace "—you can join me in the shop."

She reached for the thermos filled from a pitcher she'd grabbed that morning out of the refrigerator. One sip of the chilled water, and the telltale sweetness curled around her tongue.

Only Lacey Sweetwater Pershing could be behind the infamous matchmaking.

She hesitated, thermos poised.

On her and the mechanic?

She shook her head. The notion was beyond ridiculous.

A *Publishers Weekly* bestselling author and self-professed princess, **Chris Maday Schmidt** believes it's always the "write" time for real-life fairy tales brimming with hope for new beginnings, humor in the messy middle and heart for happy endings. Originally from the Midwest, she relocated to the Southwest with her husband and daughter. Chris writes clean and wholesome stories about family, friendship and faith for *Woman's World*, *Chicken Soup for the Soul*, *Guideposts* and Harlequin Love Inspired. Visit chrismadayschmidt.com.

Books by Chris Maday Schmidt

Love Inspired

A Father's Vow
The Fire Chief's Surprise
A Mother's Prayer

Visit the Author Profile page at LoveInspired.com.

And she called the name of the Lord
that spake unto her, Thou God seest me.
—*Genesis* 16:13

For my late daddy—the original Hank.
You set the bar, and I miss you.

Chapter One

The windshield wipers cut a swath with a rhythmic sweep to clear the heavy snowfall, but they did little to improve visibility as darkness encroached on Northern Arizona's small town of Sweetwater.

Static crackled inside the company tow, and local mechanic Hank Valentine adjusted the frequency on the radio dedicated to real-time emergency updates.

Constable Jack Wells's clipped tone barked from the speakers, raising the hair on Hank's arms.

"Got an abandoned vehicle off the state route—looks like it went down an embankment just outside town. Over."

Grabbing the receiver from its mount, Hank brought it to his mouth. "This is Big Country," he said, using the nickname he'd been given years ago. "I'm on my way. Over."

He dragged a hand over his head, exhaled hard, and cranked the wheel toward the highway.

The blizzard had hit Sweetwater—nicknamed the mile-high city in homage to Denver—with barely a warning from the weather service. That was bad enough.

But what made matters worse? Hank & Gordie's Garage, which he co-managed with his cousin, was severely short-staffed.

Not long before Jack's call came through, Hank had finally locked up—well past quitting time—with plans to cruise the side streets and head toward the wildlife preserve, just in case any residents or tourists had gotten stranded.

Thankfully, the roads had been mostly deserted, rare for a town that usually bustled with visitors.

Now, as he maneuvered the truck down Main Street—more than five thousand feet above sea level—the near-whiteout conditions that slammed into High Country earlier in the afternoon deepened the eerie quiet pressing in around him.

On Valentine's Day of all days.

He snorted. Not that it made a lick of difference to the couples cozied up at home, wrapped in candlelight and casseroles.

"Been there, done that," he muttered. No need to RSVP to a pity party for one—not when getting jilted at the altar wasn't just water under Sweetwater Lake's bridge, but a dried-up sinkhole.

Truth was, that pain went back even further—to what happened to his kid sister.

How he blamed himself… That guilt ran deep, building a wall around his heart.

Impenetrable.

Not even the town's self-appointed matchmaker's best efforts—throwing every single woman within ten miles at him like rose petals at a wedding—had made a dent.

He didn't believe he deserved love of his own. Not with the shadow still hanging over him like a storm cloud ready to break.

He shook his head and refocused. The tow truck crawled along the icy road. Even with four-wheel drive and chains, progress was slow—par for the course in the rig he and Gordie had invested in nearly twenty years ago when they first opened shop. Now he was pushing forty, wondering how life had sped by so fast.

As he passed Town Square and the bronze statue of Constance Sweetwater, the town's founder in 1864, his gaze drifted to the wooden gazebo—now a makeshift warming house beside the lazy river skating rink. The holiday cheer of December felt like a distant memory.

Flipping on his high beams, he scanned the side streets, a memory surfacing of the time he'd laced up skates a couple of winters back. Hoping to impress a new lady acquaintance, he'd let Doc Wells, the town vet, half drag him across the ice—his pride barely intact.

Jack's voice echoed in his memories: *You're gonna have to stop sabotaging relationships with your off-putting demeanor, buddy.*

Not that he was wrong. His attitude had only worsened since his fiancée walked out.

He tugged at his beard—now long enough to graze his collarbone—his fingers brushing the red-and-black flannel stretched across his chest.

Across the square, most storefronts sat dark, snow piled in gray mounds against their doors—except for Annie's Confections, Catering & Café, glowing warmly from within. The entire shop was visible through a large picture window lit like a beacon in the storm.

His eyes snapped back to the road in time to spot a lone car struggling through the intersection, its tires spinning. He pumped the brakes to avoid a collision—just as his gaze flicked back to the bakery window, where Annie Rogers wiped down a high-top table.

Hard to believe it had been just over a month since she and Fire Chief Josh celebrated their newlywed bliss on New Year's Eve.

He chuckled, remembering the groom setting off the smoke detectors to sneak a private moment with his bride, minutes before the annual cowboy boot drop in Town Square.

If anyone deserved happiness, it was those two—especially after Josh stepped up to raise his foster brother's son, left orphaned when a drunk driver killed his parents.

A familiar pang flared in Hank's gut—remorse, sharp as ever—thoughts of his sister, Rosie, always close to the surface.

But before he could spiral, a pedestrian appeared out of nowhere, crossing just a foot in front of his bumper.

"Watch out!" he shouted, heart lodging in his throat.

Startled eyes met his as the man threw up a gloved hand, then slid to safety.

Slowing to a near crawl, Hank finally reached the state route. Snow still fell in heavy sheets, but the wind had swept the pavement clear in patches, offering slightly better traction. Easing onto the gas, he steered the truck down the two-lane highway, eyes scanning the shadows cast by towering pines standing like sentinels beyond the guardrail.

Nights like this always dragged him back to *that* storm—the one when Rosie ignored his warning.

His fingers clenched the wheel, knuckles going white—just as two glowing eyes flashed in the headlights. A massive bull elk came into view, its wide rack gleaming before vanishing into the dark.

"Rosie, Rosie," he whispered, as a car rounded the bend in the opposite lane. Its high beams dipped as it passed, briefly illuminating the scattered stretch of snow between them.

Eyes pinned to the road, he kept scanning the shoulder. He'd already passed Sweetwater Lake—the town's favorite summer escape. He'd spent countless hours there, fishing rod in hand, pouring his heart out to the Lord, come rain, shine…or snow.

Farther down the highway, he'd hit the turnoff to the family ranch, the place he and Rosie had inherited after losing both parents months apart.

His jaw tightened at the memory—his kid sister storming through the house during one of her teenage outbursts, that four-year age gap between them feeling more like the width of Sweetwater Dam.

Thankfully, no other emergencies had come in. All that remained was to haul the abandoned vehicle back to the shop and catch a few hours of sleep in the garage's makeshift apartment.

His mind drifted to the ranch again. Some folks might call it abandoned now. And maybe it was. Because after burying Rosie, it was easier to sleep where the grief didn't echo so loud.

Lord, I'm tired. Help me find this car so I can catch some z's.

Movement caught his eye—a flicker. Or just a hunch.

Then again, maybe it was God's gentle nudge, redirecting him from the long list of regrets he'd rather not revisit.

Whatever it was, he'd definitely seen something. And it wasn't two thousand pounds of steel.

When he eased off the gas and adjusted the exterior lights, the swirling snow lit up just enough to reveal the glint of a fender.

He rolled forward a few more yards, then eased the truck onto a narrow pullout and flipped on the hazards.

Adrenaline surged through his veins. Had that flicker of movement been an animal seeking shelter—or searching for a meal to get through the long night?

He grabbed the blue beanie Doc Wells had gifted him during the church's Christmas exchange and tugged it over his head, same as he had before he'd quit shaving it.

After pulling on his gloves, he shoved open the driver's door. A gust of wind slammed into him, rocking the truck.

He gave a sharp whistle, the sound swallowed by the storm. Cold bit at his bare cheeks.

Not a night fit for man or beast.

But ever since Gordie talked him into co-running the garage, Hank had made it his mission to keep the town's vehicles—and by extension, its people—safe.

That was the reason behind his other nickname: Mr. Fixit.

And if he could keep even one person from Rosie's fate, maybe—just maybe—he'd outrun the memories and the guilt would dull.

Reaching back into the cab, he grabbed a flashlight from the glove box and slammed the door.

At six foot four and built like a lumberjack—or so folks liked to say—he didn't mind the cold as much as most. Still, he was glad he'd layered up in snow pants and heavy-duty boots. He'd need both to scale the snowbank.

Carefully, he tromped and slid down the ridge beside the deserted interstate, flashlight beam sweeping ahead to guide his steps. Low-hanging branches and brambles reached out like fingers, snagging at his clothes.

One brush against a pinyon pine sent a pile of snow straight down the back of his neck.

"Brr!" he muttered, flinching as the cold soaked in. His voice bounced off the canyon walls, echoing in the quiet and deepening his sense of isolation.

Except now, it wasn't just empty silence. A vast, snow-covered wilderness stretched out before him.

I will even make a way in the wilderness... He grasped on to the familiar verse as he trudged through the accumulating snow.

"I sure could use some help finding that way, Lord." Another gust of wind swept up his words.

After losing his entire family, except for his cousin, he'd felt adrift.

It wasn't until Gordie opened the garage that Hank made peace with God...and found purpose.

He had big plans to expand the business, plans that hinged on selling the ranch to finance them. But with Gordie tied up in Montana, his immediate concern was the staffing shortage.

"Thank You for a thriving business, Lord...and for Manny." The full-time mechanic had been an added blessing the past couple of weeks with Gordie out of commission. "But I could use extra hands."

Within minutes, he came across an older-model SUV jammed against the scaly bark of a juniper tree. Leaning in, he wiped slush from the passenger window and aimed his flashlight into the back seat.

Wind whipped at the tails of his flannel shirt as he spotted a tattered stuffed kitten wedged against the far door. Closer to him, a toy fire engine lay discarded on the floorboard, stirring memories of playing cars in the living room of the old ranch house.

When life was still whole.

He shoved the memories into the recesses of his battered heart and turned his attention to the hatch. Cardboard boxes and large trash bags reached the ceiling.

In the front seat, the light illuminated two bulky suitcases, a bag of dog food, and a chewed-up toy. A crumpled granola bar wrapper lay discarded in the console.

This was no abandoned vehicle.

At least, not in the traditional sense.

His heart pounded an erratic rhythm against his rib cage as his past faded into the background. He needed to stay sharp—his gut told him whoever had left the SUV couldn't be far.

Straightening, he pushed his beanie higher and scanned the area.

Maybe the driver lost control and skidded down the embankment. Or maybe car trouble forced them to pull off the main road—too far off.

He tugged at his beard, the coarse hairs stiff with frost from his breath. Even with the flashlight's beam, he couldn't make out any clear footprints—just impressions from chunks of fallen snow and a scatter of animal tracks zigzagging through the trees.

A lone coyote's cry rose above the howling wind.

His gaze jerked toward the woods, a bone-deep urgency pressing in—someone out there needed help.

If I'm not too late.

Clambering back up the slope, he yanked open the truck's passenger door and reached for the radio—then hesitated.

Instead, he pulled off a glove and fished his cell phone from his back pocket, punching in the constable's number.

Jack answered on the first ring. "Big Country! You already towed the vehicle?"

"Negative, Constable."

He paused.

Wait—

Was that a child's cry in the distance?

"I think we've got a search and rescue mission on our hands."

His gaze swung to the guardrail behind him.

Several yards beyond the abandoned vehicle…movement.

Jack's voice lost its humor. "Brief me."

"It could be wildlife. But alert the rest of the posse."

Without waiting for a response, Hank ended the call and slammed the door.

But rather than retrace his steps, he plunged through the snowdrifts piled against the guardrail and headed in the opposite direction.

"Mommy!"

There.

A child's plaintive cry echoed in the darkness. Despite the layer of flannel, gooseflesh dotted his skin.

He slipped on a patch of black ice—the cause of frequent accidents along that stretch of highway—and thrust his arms to right himself.

"Lord, You've led me this far…"

Jack would round up the rescue team—a handful of townsfolk who'd stepped up to assist the fire and police departments, already stretched thin.

Though the whiteout had eased, there was no time to wait for backup.

He stopped, cocked his head. The flashlight flickered.

Had he forgotten to charge it?

Without roadside lighting, his eyes would have to adjust to the shadows.

He shook it a couple of times. The beam flooded the forest.

If he wasn't mistaken, he was just feet from where the cry had originated.

He hoisted one leg, then the other, over the guardrail and clomped down the incline toward the unmistakable sound of voices. And…was that a growl?

Suddenly, a snarling shadow lunged from the undergrowth.

Hank raised his arms—dropping the flashlight—as a large dog froze midair, then plopped at his feet, tail wagging.

"Well, I'll be a fish out of water."

He retrieved the flashlight. Aimed the beam.

That's when he saw them.

Huddled beneath the branches of a towering pine—eyes wide with fright—two small children clung to either side of a woman. Her long hair was damp against an unbuttoned coat, the gap revealing a very pregnant belly.

He guessed the boy and girl were younger than Josie Wells, the seven-year-old daughter of the constable and Emerson, the town vet.

Unbidden, Hank's blood boiled with irritation and fear.

Questions pummeled his mind like a ticker tape parade.

What in tarnation had driven this woman into the storm?

Where did she think they were headed through the gulley?

And more importantly: How would they have survived if he hadn't found them?

He wanted to give her a piece of his mind, but bit his tongue—surprised by the crack in the wall around his heart.

"Are you a lumberjack?"

Filled with awe and excitement, the boy's voice pulled Hank from his tangled thoughts.

He met the child's wide eyes and cleared his throat—no point scaring innocent kids with the weight of his feelings.

He cleared his throat. "No, I'm not, young man. But I'm here to help you folks."

Then, without warning, the woman fainted at his feet.

This wasn't good.

Olive Hart's lids fluttered once, then twice.

That was strange.

She felt weightless—yet still braced for the bitter cold and snow to seep through her coat.

Swallowing hard, her vision sharpened, and panic welled as comprehension hit.

The gruff, hulking stranger who'd shone the flashlight in their faces now cradled her in arms as big as tree trunks.

"Is she gonna be okay, mister?"

Six-year-old Simon's voice filtered through the cotton balls that had replaced all rational thought since they'd set out that morning.

Olive's heart pinched at the worry woven into Simon's voice. They didn't need one more thing to fret over, not after everything the three of them, Roman included, had weathered these past six months.

Still, the family Lab treated the day's ordeal like a grand adventure ending in a broken-down vehicle.

So much for the mechanical know-how her granddad had passed down during those long summers when her mom left her at his homestead and disappeared until school started again in the fall.

She forced a smile into her voice.

"Momma will be fine, son. Now, please put me down, sir."

The man snorted—clear proof her bravado had missed the mark, especially after her fainting spell at his feet.

"That's not his name, Mommy."

How long had she been unconscious?

Three-year-old Holly gently brushed a mittened hand over the tangled hair slipping down Olive's shoulder and whispered in her ear, "His name is Mr. Big."

Without a word, the large man set her on her feet atop the packed snow.

He studied the four of them in the flashlight's glow, and though he said nothing, the furrow in his brow hinted at thoughts she couldn't begin to read.

"If I think you're gonna pass out again, I'm carrying you out of here."

His jaw clenched, and she could practically see the gears turning beneath a beanie that didn't stop his ginger-tinted beard from frosting over.

Splaying a gloved hand over her rounded abdomen, she noticed his eyes track the subtle movement.

She was nearly thirty weeks along and chalked the fainting up to low blood sugar—even though she had a granola bar for breakfast.

How long ago had that been?

"Mister—"

"Hank Valentine, ma'am."

"He looks like Paul Bunyan, don't he, Mom?"

Simon tugged on her coattail, and she patted his head, releasing a long sigh.

This day was unfolding in ways she never could've imagined.

"Mister Valentine—Hank—our car broke down and—"

The man tugged on his beard with a hand the size of a salad plate, then grunted.

"Let's get you to my truck and go from there."

He hoisted a child under each arm like they weighed no more than sacks of potatoes, then nodded toward the dog—still wagging its tail like they were headed to a party.

Lord, I don't have it in me to question this man's intentions.

If Roman was okay, that had to be enough for now.

She grabbed the Lab's leash and trudged after the man, doing her best to step into his massive boot prints without losing her balance.

By then, the wind and snow had subsided, making the trek back to where the SUV had gone down easier.

"Oh wow, Mom, look!"

Simon pointed at a tow truck parked just past the patch of road where they'd slid when they'd pulled off the state route.

But would there be enough room for all of them?

Once they reached the vehicle, the man called Big Country set Simon and Holly on the ground with a care that belied his size. When he opened the back door to reveal a full bench seat, her pulse began to steady—until she spotted the space where Holly's car seat should have been.

"Closest thing I've got is a booster seat left behind from a recent tow," Hank said, pulling it from behind the seat. "Not perfect, but better than nothing."

Olive nodded and whispered a silent prayer as Hank buckled her daughter in place.

Roman hopped onto the seat between the kids, curled his tail around his legs, and let out a soft *whuff.*

Hank closed the door, rounded the cab, and glanced pointedly at her belly.

"You need a lift?"

Despite the near-freezing temps, heat crawled up her neck.

"I can manage."

But when her heel slipped off the top step, strong hands caught her by the waist.

With a quick boost, he helped her into the passenger seat and shut the door behind her.

Familiar feelings of being a burden crept in, but she was too cold and too tired to think of a way to repay his kindness.

Seconds ticked by as he brushed snow from the windshield, followed by a muffled, one-sided phone call she couldn't make out.

Then the driver's door swung open, and the lumberjack with the fitting nickname climbed in.

He buckled up, and in the brief glow of the overhead light, she took him in—his clear blue eyes, the deep grooves that fanned across weathered skin. Melted snow streaked his ginger beard with silver, and his flannel shirt stretched across a barrel chest built for heavy lifting and long days.

After flipping the heater to high, he leaned over and pulled the seat belt across her abdomen, clicking it into place with a soft snap.

She swallowed, the knot of anxiety loosening as her nerves settled—like calm waters frozen over, given the weather.

"Who were you talking to?"

She clasped her gloved hands in her lap, the question an attempt at normalcy in a day that had been anything but.

So much for treating the kids to a special Valentine's Day.

Her heart squeezed with guilt—for Simon and Holly, for the choices that had brought them here. But there'd be time later to unpack all the feelings she'd tried to leave behind in the house that used to be their home in Snowpeak.

Right now, her only goal was getting to their destination—and praying the big man behind the wheel would be willing to help them the rest of the way.

Once they were warm, dry, and settled into their new home, she'd figure out how to thank him.

She glanced into the back seat, where both kids watched the man behind the wheel with wide-eyed wonder. Roman lay curled between them, tail thumping gently.

The man grunted again, then turned the key in the ignition. After a quick check for traffic, he gave it gas and pulled onto the road.

"Called off the rescue posse," he mumbled. He shot her a brief look. "Where to?"

"Wait—what about my car? Our belongings?"

She leaned forward, seat belt pulling tight across her stomach, and stared into the forest that had felt much scarier before God sent a pseudo-lumberjack tow truck driver to their rescue.

"I'll get it later—after putting you up in town."

His tone brooked no argument.

He executed a sharp three-point turn, then steered the truck toward Sweetwater.

And the fresh start Olive prayed was waiting there.

"I think you should get checked out at Sweetwater General first."

His eyes stayed fixed on the road, and she willed her pulse to slow, trying to weave a calm she didn't feel into her voice.

She had little funds for a hospital visit—not after her ex-husband had left them high and dry.

"I really think I just need some food and a good night's sleep."

Her gaze drifted to the shadows outside the window, and a

shiver ran through her as she remembered how scared she'd been when the car had careened off the road.

The original plan had been to climb the embankment and walk alongside the guardrail. But she worried another vehicle might lose control and plow into them. So they'd huddled beneath outstretched tree limbs, sheltering from the storm.

That's when she remembered the Biblical story of Hagar and her son Ishmael—how Hagar had questioned if God had abandoned them.

But when rescue came moments later, her chest warmed with a spark of hope.

You're the God who sees me.

"...do I take you?"

The tow truck slowed as the state route funneled into the small town that would be their home until after the baby was born—after which she'd decide if staying would be permanent.

She observed the recently plowed streets, their edges lined with mounds of snow. Sidewalks lay deserted, a quiet stillness blanketing the small town. Nervous anticipation coursed through her veins, mixing with the hushed whispers of her children that carried into the front seat.

Roman barked and tried to wriggle his way into the cab.

Startled, she realized she'd zoned out.

"Roman, sit—and Annie's Confections, Catering & Café, sir...er, Hank." She licked lips chapped from the cold. "If it's no bother."

The man tugged on his beard with one beefy hand as he turned onto what appeared to be the town's main drag.

"You sure? Don't think she'll be open this late."

"She's expecting us. We're the new tenants in the studio apartment above the shop."

At least, that's what the director of Hope House had arranged with the bakery owner. Along with a part-time job.

She realized the back seat had turned quiet and peeked over her shoulder. Simon and Holly melted against each other, faces slack in slumber. Roman sprawled across them, big head tucked between his front legs.

Thank You, Lord.

The silent prayer tumbled from her lips—a spark of gratitude that gently lifted her deflated spirits. Like a hand pump adding air to a flat tire, while it didn't fix everything, it helped her stay upright.

When the tow truck bumped against the curb in front of the only business still glowing from within, the sleet and snow had shifted to sporadic flakes that drifted through the air without a care.

"So Annie knows about your car troubles?"

Hank shifted into Park, then turned toward her. The weariness in his eyes—as if he carried burdens of his own—tugged at her conscience. Her midsection clenched with guilt, knowing she might be adding to his day…for all she knew, he was taking time away from a wife and kids to help her out.

She willed her heartbeat to slow. "I—yes. But my cell phone died earlier…"

Mentally, she acknowledged the wisdom of a backup plan.

He gave a curt nod, then unbuckled and opened his door. A gust of icy air whooshed in before it slammed shut again.

By the time he rounded the front of the truck and reached her side, she'd already unfastened her seat belt.

Without preamble, he opened her door and lifted her easily into his arms. Her breath caught—not from fear, but from the gentleness of the gesture.

With care, he set her on the cleared walkway in front of the bakery entrance, then motioned her ahead.

Roman's large head lifted, eyebrows twitching with curiosity. In a single leap, he cleared the console and landed at Olive's feet. She looped his leash around one of the old-fashioned lampposts lining the parking strip, the metal cold beneath her fingers.

Behind her, Hank carefully retrieved her sleeping children from the truck.

The bells above the bakery door tinkled as they stepped inside.

Warmth greeted them first, followed by the comforting scent of yeast and spice—like cinnamon rolls fresh from the oven. It wrapped around her like a hug and reminded her, with a pang, that she hadn't eaten for hours.

An attractive woman, in her late twenties, close to Olive's age, swooped through a pair of swinging café doors. Her dark blond hair was piled into a messy topknot, and black-framed glasses perched on the bridge of her nose. A white apron tied around her waist bore the shop's name in bold pink letters.

"You made it!" Relief sparkled in her blue-gray eyes as she blew an errant strand of hair off her forehead.

She hurried from behind the counter and pulled Olive into a quick, unexpected hug.

"I'm sorry we're so late," Olive murmured, caught off guard by the sincere welcome.

As she stepped back, the soothing scent of cinnamon and vanilla clung to the woman, who could only be Annie.

"Nonsense," she said with a dismissive wave. "I'm just glad you're here, safe and sound."

Annie turned to the man holding Simon and Holly and adjusted her glasses. "Got your hands full there, Hank?"

"Uh…where do you want me to…"

He looked ready to bolt, and Olive couldn't blame him—not when she'd felt like such a burden after Donny divorced her and left her and the kids in financial ruin.

She and Annie reached for the children just as their eyes blinked open. Hank gently lowered them to the floor, then blew out a sharp breath and caught her in his blue-eyed gaze.

"Okay if I bring back your essentials and tow your car to the garage?"

She nodded, too tired to form the words her heart longed to say. "Thank you."

Her once-cheerful disposition had seen better days, but it lifted—just a little.

At least she had three months to figure out how to pay for the repairs.

By then, her baby would be born.

Hank bobbed his head, then slipped out the bakery door—the bells jingling in his wake.

"I'm hungry, Mommy."

"Me too."

Annie grinned and gave each child's nose a gentle tweak. "Miss Annie's got you covered."

"Oh, I really can't impose any more—" Olive's protest faltered as her stomach betrayed her with a loud growl.

Annie chuckled. "Nonsense." But the smile faded, replaced by a faint frown. "Besides, this gives me a chance to break the latest news before Hank returns."

Olive's pulse skipped. She steeled herself against the unease rising in her chest.

Lord, I'm not sure I can take much more.

The hunger pangs in Olive's stomach twisted into a bundle of nerves as her gaze drifted to the bakery windows—and her reflection. The sight of her pale skin and caramel-brown hair clinging to her head testified to the harrowing day the four of them had experienced thus far.

Then her heart jolted. The lamppost outside was empty.

"Roman!"

Annie gently patted her shoulder. "It's okay. Hank untied him and let him into the tow truck."

Olive blinked.

Roman was usually friendly with everyone, but he'd always been indifferent to Donny. And Hank? A stranger. Yet the dog followed him without hesitation.

"Don't let Hank's surly attitude fool you," Annie said, her lips curving into a soft smile. "He may be as big as a country—and built like a grizzly—but deep down, he's got the heart of a teddy bear." She hesitated. "It's just…nights like this are extra hard for him."

Olive nodded, feigning understanding, though Annie's words didn't quite connect. Still, she was no stranger to life's struggles.

"What did you need to tell me?" she asked softly.

"Let's get some food in you first. Then we'll talk."

Before long, Olive patted her rounded belly, comforted by thick slabs of grilled potato bread oozing with cheese and bowls of steaming, chunky tomato soup. At some point, she may have even nodded off.

Until Annie's voice pierced her dreamlike state.

"I'm so sorry, but the heat in the upstairs apartment went out this afternoon."

Olive blinked, trying to register her words.

"I'm afraid you can't stay there until the furnace is fixed."

The bells above the bakery door jingled just then, drawing her gaze. Hank stepped inside, suitcases dangling from each hand, a bag of dog food clutched beneath one arm.

Black spots clouded her vision. She swayed.

And for the third time that evening, she felt herself swept up into two massive arms.

Chapter Two

Three times in a matter of hours, Hank had breathed in that sharp pine scent laced with something floral—prickly and sweet, like the woman named Olive Hart.

Less than sixty minutes earlier, he'd escaped the bakery, the family's dog an eager companion by his side. His return trip along the state route had been a piece of cake since the storm had tapered.

Getting the SUV out hadn't exactly been easy—more like a wrestling match with mud and a stubborn axle.

Now, with both vehicles parked in front of the bakery, he did his best to occupy the subdued, well-behaved children. Goofy drawings sketched on napkins and crumbs from the bakery's infamous sweet and sour lemon bars littered the surface of the high-top table.

A small hand tugged on his shirtsleeve, a distraction from the muffled voices that carried from the kitchen.

"When's Mommy coming out?"

Little Holly's golden-hued eyes—so much like her mother's—searched his face, wide with trust.

He sucked in a hefty breath, then exhaled to buy time. What was he supposed to tell the child?

"Has the chief ever put out a huge fire?" Simon looked up from his stick figure drawing of a dog.

He pictured the black Lab he'd left curled on the front seat, heater on full blast, and a chew toy to occupy him.

Hank ruffled the boy's mop of caramel-colored hair that fell across eyes a shade darker than his little sister's. "You can ask Mr. Josh sometime."

Simon nodded, then went back to his sketch.

Just then, Annie pushed through the swinging café doors, a smile on her face. Whether the smile was for the children's sake or his, there was no denying Olive's latest episode had affected him more than he cared to admit.

"Miss Annie, Miss Annie!" Holly bounced on her chair.

"Your mommy will be just fine, sweetie. And she'll be out as soon as Fire Chief Josh gives the okay."

As she enveloped both children in a warm hug, she winked at Hank over their heads, and relief washed over him.

After Olive had regained consciousness this last time, she'd again refused a trip to the ER. But she reluctantly agreed to be examined by the fire chief.

He tugged on his beard as he watched Simon and Holly. Annie had told him the Harts were being displaced from the apartment due to a broken-down furnace. He'd offered to check it out, but she'd insisted he keep the kids company so Annie could support Olive.

"So there's no room at the inn, then?" His response mirrored the age-old Bible story, with Olive's situation similar to the expectant Mary, sans a donkey and husband in tow.

Annie straightened and shook her head. "According to Lacey, the B and B's at capacity because of Valentine's Day."

"Valentine's!" Holly displayed a crude drawing of a heart on her napkin.

"Oh, honey, that's lovely." Annie brushed a hand over the girl's flyaway hairs. "You can give it to your mommy when she comes out."

Another crack splintered through the fortress that had long encased Hank's heart. The image of his empty ranch house flashed in his mind—and with it, the ache of old dreams buried under years of silence.

He tipped his head back, eyes on the ceiling.

Lord, just a tiny reminder: I fix things—not people.

He couldn't remember the last time he'd stepped into the home he'd hung on to for more years than necessary.

Though he still paid Miss Marie to keep it clean—"just in case"—his pantry and refrigerator were no doubt as bare as Old Mrs. Hubbard's.

Yet the Lord's prompting was clear.

"Promise you'll check in at the clinic this week, or at least with Emerson Wells, the constable's wife and our trusted vet." Fire Chief Josh held the café doors open for Olive and chuckled.

"She may not deliver human babies, but she's a pro with the four-legged variety."

Olive's sudden giggle drew him in, and he couldn't stop staring. She'd removed her knit hat and coat. Silky waves tumbled over her shoulders. An oversized sweatshirt did nothing to hide her pregnancy; denim jeans were tucked into a pair of worn winter boots.

But it was the different shades of brown and gold in her curls that caused him to gawk.

"Mommy!" The children bolted from their chairs to wrap their arms around Olive's legs.

Their trio of love was almost tangible. The same kind of love he once had dreamed of.

But he told himself an invitation to stay overnight at the ranch was not a marriage proposal.

Eyes once guarded now sparked with hope. The woman amazed him with her resilience despite her circumstances.

He stood and rose to his full height.

"It's just me at the ranch…your family can stay there."

Olive gave an adamant shake of her head.

"Thank you, but I, we…"

The woman was outnumbered. She had no idea who she was up against.

And after a bit of convincing from the adults, she conceded.

Whether exhaustion or desperation had tipped the scales—or both—it took little time for the five of them to get back on the road.

"Do you have a hatchet?"

"How many trees do you have?"

"Are there cows and pigs on your ranch?"

"Do you have a blue ox?"

How much sugar did they manage to eat?

"Simon, Holly. Enough questions for Mr.—Hank."

Olive's tone served its purpose, and silence accompanied the rest of the drive.

While the Harts got settled in the guest suite in the rear of the sprawling rambler, he stored their belongings in an old shed near the stalls. When he and Rosie were young, those stalls contained horses, chickens, and cows.

He swallowed the lump in his throat. Back on his property for the first time in a while, the lingering scent of fresh-cut hay and rich loam hit him hard—along with a wheelbarrow full of regret for how he'd failed his sister.

It wouldn't be easy being there.

But he had work in the morning. And he'd promised Olive that he'd tow her car to the shop first thing.

He'd wanted to take it to the garage once he'd dropped her brood off. But the chief had pulled him aside while the Harts piled into his truck.

Despite Josh's assurances that Olive's vitals were strong, he encouraged Hank to spend the night at the ranch.

So instead, after stowing their boxes, he unhitched her car and took the truck into town to pick up a few essentials at the market.

And maybe his presence on the property would allow the woman to sleep.

He told himself that circumstances had a way of looking better in the morning. Something about the mercies of God renewing every day.

Except the Lord had different plans.

When Sunday morning dawned, it started with a high volume of tow calls.

Olive had mentioned the possibility of attending church in the morning. But when he apologized, she simply asked for the Bible stashed in the SUV's glove box.

Once he pulled the dog-eared leather book from her vehicle, its margins filled with wavery penmanship, he sensed how much it meant to the expectant mother.

After word of the new arrivals spread through the congregation, several parishioners showed up bearing goodwill and supplies.

That evening, Olive served a homemade casserole Mrs. Spagnoletti—the wife of the former town councilman—had delivered.

With a smile that had brightened since the night before, Olive told Hank about the toys, books, and even a few maternity outfits the ladies had brought. Still, he hadn't missed the faint tension shadowing the delicate skin at her temples.

It wasn't until he retired early after an exhausting day—his head just hitting the pillow when Gordie called—that Hank momentarily questioned a faith it had taken years to rebuild.

"Hey, cousin, I'm afraid things are worse off here than we anticipated and—"

Gordie paused mid-sentence, the kind of silence that reminded Hank of the calm before a storm. He braced himself.

"I hate to do this to you, but I'll be out of commission for another three months."

Of course, he couldn't say no. At least he still had Manny at the garage. But the cars had been piling up in the shop—literally—and included a late-model SUV that belonged to a certain expectant mother without wheels.

Even more troubling?

Figuring out how he was supposed to handle Olive and her brood from here on out—because as long as the furnace in the bakery apartment stayed busted, one night of accommodations could easily turn into an open-ended arrangement.

And while it wasn't technically his job to fix the thing, the part of him that answered to "Mr. Fixit" didn't want to let it slide.

But the snow and the shop backlog had his hands tied.

Hushed whispers tugged at his sleep, and tiny fingers poked at the beard grazing his collarbone, pulling Hank from a recurring dream he'd long classified as a nightmare.

Though less frequent over the years, those dreams always returned with the snow—hauling him back to the scene of his sister's accident whenever a storm blew through town.

Now, however, the scents of fresh-brewed coffee and maple syrup merged with matching giggles.

Pretending to growl like a grizzly bear, he clasped two wriggling bodies against his chest to produce a cacophony of squeals in the morning's dawn.

Surprisingly nimble on her feet—at least in his estimation—Olive appeared outside his room within seconds, her pretty face flushed and her eyes flashing with concern that seemed a bit out of proportion to the kids' playful antics. Then again, he knew his size could be intimidating to strangers.

Releasing his loose grip on the children, he wrestled with the unfamiliar feelings that tried to stake a claim behind his rib cage as the miniature humans scurried to their mother's side, heads bowed low.

"I'm so sorry—these two never should've been in your room, let alone bothering you." Placing a gentle hand on both heads and bending to their level, she whispered something before they scampered down the hallway. Without waiting for a response, Olive averted her eyes as she pushed his door closed.

Alone with his thoughts again, he tugged on his beard, the wheels in his brain attempting to make sense of the past couple of days.

After Annie had confirmed her call for furnace repair, it hadn't made sense to move Olive and her brood to the B and B when they were already set up in his home, so one night of hosting guests had transitioned into two.

Tossing the bedcovers aside, he hoisted himself to his feet. He left the shade shut since the morning light had yet to reach the canyon where the ranch was situated. But as the trill of laughter carried to his room, he halted with one leg shoved into his coveralls.

Who am I trying to kid?

He couldn't deny the warm feelings accompanying the pitter-patter of small feet filling the old homestead, or after he pulled into the carport and entered the mudroom to catch the whiff of a home-cooked meal. All while reminding himself that it was a temporary arrangement, even as his heart betrayed him with long-held hopes buried with his family.

Not that a woman like Olive would ever find herself interested in a broken mechanic. Snorting at the irony, he zipped up his work clothes then exited the bedroom.

As he padded down the hallway in his stocking feet, his stomach rumbled before he even reached the kitchen. The oval wooden table—once surrounded by his own family—was now crowded with serving dishes piled high with waffles, fresh preserves, and a steaming egg-and-sausage hot dish.

Olive stood at the sink, her back to him, arms submerged in sudsy water up to her elbows—her attention fixed on the window where the sky was breaking into a dull gray.

"Mr. Big!" Simon looked up from his spot on the sofa, where he sat next to his sister with a book spread open across their laps, and Roman wedged between them, his big black head tucked between his front legs.

The domesticity of the scene unfolding before him threatened to buckle his resolve to stay indifferent to the family's problems—though deep down, he suspected it might already be too late.

He coughed into the back of his hand to clear the emotion stuck in his throat, then gave the kids a quick wave as Olive turned, their eyes meeting.

"Good morning," he said, adding a smile to mask the gruffness in his voice.

She returned his smile and wiped her hands on an embroidered Gone Fishin' dish towel handcrafted by Annie as a donation to the most recent Christmas Boutique, then nodded toward the table.

"Help yourself. We have plenty more where that came from—thanks to your congregation's generosity."

Her golden eyes twinkled—a sight he preferred to the worry that often clouded them.

"Um, Hank…?"

Tucking a caramel-colored curl into an elastic band that held back her hair and gave her a youthful appearance that stirred up his emotions even more, she approached the table. He blinked, then scooped the mouthwatering selection of food onto his plate.

"Yes?" He pointed at the table. "Thank you for this, by the way."

She gripped the back of a chair with both hands. "It's the least I could do, but…"

He sensed her discomfort, then realized he'd neglected to update her on her vehicle, though it wasn't the news he'd been hoping to spring on her.

With his foot, he nudged a chair away from the table. "Have a seat."

Chewing on her bottom lip, she perched on the edge and clasped her fingers atop her ample belly.

"I was wonder—"

"I need to order—"

Their voices collided, eliciting an awkward chuckle to pass between them.

"You first," she said as she poured herself a glass of iced water from a pitcher in the center of the table.

He cleared his throat. "I'm waiting on parts for your car—so until they come in, I'll take you and the kids where you need to go." He'd left a note for Manny to find the necessary parts for her older-model vehicle.

But his offer to serve as her chauffeur had popped out of nowhere.

If You could clone me about now, Lord.

Olive had taken a sip from her glass, and her expressive eyes sparked with curiosity.

Hank realized the pitcher must contain sweet water Lacey Pershing had brought over from the inn's proprietary aquifer. Leave it to the councilman's wife to take advantage of any opportunity to play matchmaker.

He stifled a grunt as she refocused on him and shook her head. "We already owe you too much, I couldn't possibly impose any—"

"The matter's settled. And if I'm not mistaken, Annie invited you to drop by the bakery when you're up to it."

He popped a flaky croissant into his mouth and groaned, ignoring Olive's *harrumph*.

"So you and the kids be ready to leave in fifteen."

That was how the two of them ended up at Annie's Confections, Catering & Café, after Olive had registered both children in the preschool-through-second-grade program at Sweetwater Community Church. And where Lacey's husband and town councilman, Drew Pershing—Persh to everyone who knew him—approached them.

The man swiped at his short-cropped goatee before extending a hand. "I'm so glad to meet you, Ms. Hart."

She returned his greeting, then shrugged out of her coat. "You, too, Councilman, but please, call me Olive."

Persh nodded. "All my friends call me Persh." Flashing a grin, he clapped Hank on the shoulder. "Hey, old man—you better have told our newest resident about dinner at the B and B on Friday."

Hank snorted and tugged on his beard, eyes snapping to Olive's—hers glimmered with interest.

"I'm guessing she knows now."

* * *

"Don't worry, it's nothing fancy." Annie adjusted her black frames, accentuating blue-gray eyes, then glanced at Olive's midsection. "You sure you're feeling up to seeing the bakery in action?"

By then, Hank and Persh had left the shop mid-conversation about the weather. A lone customer clacked away on a laptop keyboard at one of the high-top tables; a half-eaten wedge of biscotti teetered on the edge of a plate beside a steaming cup of hazelnut coffee.

"Absolutely." Olive smiled at her new boss. "And no more fainting spells." She couldn't even remember the last time she'd slept two consecutive nights without waking except to use the restroom.

Thank You, Lord, for small blessings. Hank's grizzly bear appearance popped into her mind. *And very large ones.*

"Okay, then, why don't you shadow me to start?" Annie tightened her apron ties behind her back, then held up a finger. "Hold on, you'll need one of these."

As the baker scurried behind the counter and through the swinging café doors, Olive perused the well-appointed, charming space. Throughout the shop, bold pink accents complemented the black-and-white-checked tiles, and an old-fashioned soda machine graced one end of the counter.

Identical glass cases provided bird's-eye views of various sweet and savory sundries for purchase. She'd barely registered the bakery's offerings the night she and the children had first arrived. How had two days already passed since Hank had come to their rescue?

"Here you are." Annie extended an apron identical to hers.

After securing it around a waist that had seen better days, she smoothed the material against her belly.

"I don't believe I thanked you, Annie, for your work with Hope House." When Donny had deserted their little family, he'd also let their home fall into foreclosure. So if not for the arrangement between the baker and the pregnancy resource center in Olive's hometown, the four of them faced the possibility of life in a shelter.

Which would've happened had Hank not offered lodging at his ranch.

Annie brushed off her comment with a shrug. "It's no secret that Eileen, the nonprofit's director, came to my assistance when I was a scared and pregnant teenager." A wistful smile played across her mouth. "And I've been supporting Hope House ever since."

Further conversation was interrupted when the chimes over the door jingled, and in strode the fire chief; a dark-haired boy, she guessed around fifteen months, preceded him. Arms outstretched, the toddler shuffled toward Annie. "Mommy up! Pwease!"

A wide grin split the baker's face as she scooped him against her chest. And when he buried his head against her neck, she showered his fine hair with kisses.

Olive thought of the new life growing within her. The one that her ex-husband had abandoned—along with the rest of his family—the burden being "too much" for Donny.

Which had validated her beliefs that reached clear back to the beginning, ever since her twin sister had died at birth.

Correction: from the time my father disappeared from our lives.

Even as a child, she'd felt the sting of her mother's blame—like Olive was the reason her father left, or her twin sister died. No wonder she'd grown up believing she was a burden to everyone.

But never Granddad. She'd always known she was loved unconditionally by her maternal grandfather. Her heart squeezed as she pictured his bushy silver eyebrows and knobby knuckles from arthritis.

"Glad to see color on your face—Olive, right?" Dressed in civilian clothes, Josh Rogers offered a warm smile bracketed by a faint beard that shadowed his jaw. Although a tall man, she couldn't help but compare him to the man called Big Country, who appeared larger than life.

"Yes, and thank you, Chief." She chuckled. "No doubt a result of the expert care I received the other night."

Laughing, he sidled up to Annie to plant a chaste kiss on her forehead. "And hello to you, my beautiful wife."

"Olive, you've already met my sweet-talking husband…" She side-eyed Josh before setting the little boy onto the floor. Without a second thought, he toddled over to the glass cases.

"And that," she said, pointing toward the energetic youngster, "is our son, Finn."

The fire chief splayed his palm across his wife's stomach and lowered his voice. "And *this* is his little brother or sister." He winked, then scooted away from Annie just in time to avoid the swat she aimed at his bicep.

"We've only shared the news with a few of our friends, since I'm still in the first trimester…"

She tracked her husband, who'd joined Finn near a door that Annie told her led into the café expansion completed the previous fall.

"But apparently Josh isn't too concerned." She giggled. "Although small-town gossip will spread like wildfire if it hasn't already."

Olive grinned as she cupped her palms around her own abdomen. "It won't be long before you can't hide it anyway."

"I forget—you're around thirty weeks, right?"

She nodded as Annie ushered her behind the counter.

"Yes, and I'd be grateful if you could recommend an obstetrician in town." It would be another week before she received her first paycheck to cover the medical expense. But at least food and shelter were taken care of for now.

"Of course. I'll get you that info before Hank picks you up."

Once the fire chief and their son had said their goodbyes, the rest of the morning zipped by while Annie instructed her on using the ancient cash register, then walked her through several transactions, and the no-nonsense procedures for opening the store.

The flurry of nonstop activity had left little time for Olive to ruminate on her earlier fright, when Simon and Holly had sneaked into Hank's private sanctuary and "poked the bear"—a saying some used, and one that seemed fitting for him.

Mortification had dogged her heels as she'd rounded up the two instigators, half-expecting Hank to insist they find alternate arrangements without passing go, as if her family were living out a real-life game of Monopoly. Though nothing about their situation resembled any game she'd choose to play.

Never mind the sweet and innocent picture the three roughhousers had made, resulting in a funny hitch to her pulse before she'd shooed the children from his room.

"So how's life on the ranch?"

Olive blinked, pulled from her thoughts. Her gaze drifted to the source of the warm, citrusy scent filling the bakery as Annie pulled a baking pan from a newer model oven—one Olive had learned had recently replaced the former mainstay affectionately dubbed "Old Betsy"—then set a fresh batch of her specialty sweet and sour lemon bars onto a rack to cool.

At first, she'd felt awkward—and more than a little guilty for inconveniencing Hank. But the ranch was…comfortable, almost like they belonged.

Grabbing a pair of oven mitts, she retrieved a second pan from the oven, the tangy citrus fragrance infusing the small space as she shoved the silly notion aside. It was only a matter of time until they wore out their welcome.

Her ex-husband's face flitted across her mind's eye. Not only had she and the children—and her sick granddad—been more than he'd signed up for, but Donny had also sought companionship outside of their marriage, which only added insult to injury.

As she contemplated her response, she placed the pan on a second cooling rack and followed Annie to the farmhouse sink. After removing the oven mitts, she picked up an embroidered towel like the one at the ranch and dried the dishes Annie had washed.

"It's been easier than I expected," she said. In fact, when Hank hadn't turned them away, she'd said a prayer that he'd welcome them to stay as long as she kept the table stocked with food and the kids and dog out of his hair, until the apartment's heating was fixed and they'd move upstairs.

Annie peeked at her, a thoughtful expression reflected behind her lenses. "I'm glad. He really is one of the best…besides the fire chief, of course."

She nudged Olive's shoulder with hers. "I'm not sure if Hank's shared his story with you, but it might help to know he's experienced his measure of loss—"

Olive recalled Annie telling her the night they'd arrived at the bakery that this time of year was especially difficult for him. And despite his grumpy manner, she'd sensed a kindred spirit while wrestling with her own grief.

Pausing mid-scrub, Annie pinned her with her gaze.

"Of course it's not my place to say, but I hope you can look past his gruff exterior."

Though she couldn't begin to guess what trials the big man had faced, Olive was more determined than ever to lighten the load he'd taken on by opening his home to her family.

Hours later, she'd craned her neck from the passenger seat of Hank's tow truck, heat prickling along her neckline as she'd leveled a look at Simon and Holly to hush the nonstop chatter.

"And then Miss Marie gave us hot choc'late and the teacher said—"

"… Pastor Mark prayed in class and—"

"Kids."

When a large hand patted her knee, she jerked and swung her gaze to Hank.

"They're excited, let them talk."

Who was this grizzly man showing the heart of a teddy bear?

At least, that's how Annie had described him. And after what she'd seen with her own two eyes the past few days, it was hard not to believe it.

Despite—or maybe because of—the steady babbling from the back seat, the drive ended quickly. Soon, they'd turned onto the long road leading to the ranch house.

Tightening her scarf, Olive had studied the freshly plowed lane. From what she'd gathered while chatting with the parishioners—who'd shown up in droves from the local church, a kindness that touched her deeply and added yet another item to her growing list of debts to repay—the temperatures had been colder than normal. But at least the streets and walkways had been cleared for safe passage.

The days that followed blurred together, marked only by that first chaotic afternoon—Roman had gotten into both bathrooms, leaving evidence of his antics strung through the hallways and across the living space.

Hank had grumbled at first, then enlisted Simon and Holly's assistance to round up the rolls of toilet paper while entertaining them with stories of his childhood and getting caught tossing tissue in the trees at a neighboring ranch. Eyes wide as saucers, his helpers had giggled, while the naughty Lab trailed them from room to room.

Now, early Thursday afternoon, she chuckled at the memory as she wiped down the table at the ranch, waiting for Hank to drop off her kids. Though she was only scheduled part-time, she'd already met several staff members—including Carley, whose pixie haircut was streaked with vibrant red for Valentine's Day—and a few community college students who worked there.

So when the echo of boots rose from the mudroom, she'd expected Hank to follow.

Instead, Miss Marie—the part-time receptionist for the church and private school and, from what she'd been told, the town matriarch who also worked as bookkeeper for the Sweetwater Bed & Breakfast—entered the kitchen between Holly and Simon.

"Hello, dear. It's my regular cleaning day, so I thought I'd save Hank a trip." Smile lines fanned out from hazel eyes.

"Miss Marie, I've already given the place a good scrubbing—" She waved her hand toward the spotless kitchen and great room. "It's the least I can do."

"Mommy, can we have a snack?" Simon piped up, letting his coat fall to the floor at his feet, one stocking close to falling off.

"As soon as you hang up your jacket where it belongs." She shook her head as she ushered Miss Marie to a dining chair. Center stage, a wooden board featured a selection of sliced cheeses and meats, butter crackers, plump purple grapes, wedges of pineapple, and apple slices.

"Thank you, dear. But it's your day off, and Big Country certainly doesn't expect you to keep house—not when he's helping your family."

While the kids climbed onto the chairs and she plated the fresh fruit, meats, cheeses, and crackers, she considered Miss Marie's words.

She remembered Hank's admission upon their arrival—that he was a fixer by nature.

Was that his plan?

To fix her family like they were a project? And then what?

She'd walked that road most of her life.

Granddad had never treated her like that, though. Maybe he'd tried to make up for her mother's hands-off approach, but he'd taught her about God—the One who could mend, heal, and repair—and how to keep a car running.

But worse than feeling like a burden was believing Hank saw them as a problem to solve.

Which won't happen if I have anything to say about it.

The next evening couldn't come soon enough—especially after Annie broke the news about the furnace repair backlog and her refusal to let Olive's family move into the apartment until the heat was fixed.

So she planned to pull Lacey Pershing aside to ask about the availability of a cottage she'd seen in a brochure near the bakery entrance. Surely Lacey would agree to let her clean in exchange for room and board—as long as the inn allowed pets.

She excused Simon and Holly from the table, then responded absently, "He's been nothing but a good sport."

After a sweet visit with Miss Marie, Olive helped Simon and Holly finish their school drawings of their favorite things, tucked them in tight, and pulled out *Paul Bunyan*—a nightly tradition since being rescued by their very own pseudo lumberjack.

Both kids drifted off, and she padded to the kitchen to pack away the dinner leftovers—an idea forming for how she might repay Hank for his kindness.

She nearly jumped out of her skin. "Hank!"

The man she'd been thinking about sat at the table, mid-bite, cheeks blooming pink like he'd been caught sneaking cookies from the jar.

He swallowed quickly and stood. "Sorry—I called it an early night."

She fanned the air with one hand. "No need to apologize. Sit, finish. You've earned it." Sliding into a chair, she offered a cheerful smile. "I was thinking… I'd like to help at the garage until my car's back in action."

His expression hardened. "No."

Her smile faltered. "But I can—"

He sliced the air with one hand, his tone as firm as his jaw. "End of story."

Well. That went sideways fast.

She blinked against the sting in her eyes and rose too quickly, the chair legs scraping. Without another word, she fled down the hallway, heart thudding against her ribs.

Of all the stubborn, mule-headed, maddening men.

Slipping beneath the covers beside the children moments later, she tugged the blanket up to her chin. Roman hopped onto the foot of the bed with a soft thump, circling once before settling in, his warm weight a comfort against her feet.

She sighed, the tension in her chest loosening as she clutched her grandfather's worn leather Bible close. Once again, she'd forgotten to ask Hank for an update on her SUV. But that could wait.

You see me, Lord. Her heart whispered the words as her eyes fluttered, then closed. *And I trust You have a plan.*

Sleep was restless, the little one inside her doing somersaults.

But they'd made it this far—and despite Hank's pigheadedness, she wasn't about to give up now.

Chapter Three

"Parts for Ms. Hart's SUV are on order," said Manny Ortega, Hank's full-time mechanic, consulting a list scribbled on the back of a bakery receipt.

Given Hank had been spoiled with homemade lunches all week, the receipt probably dated back to before Olive and her family arrived.

He released a pent-up breath and craned his neck to scan the calendar tacked on the wall over his shoulder. With mid-February behind them, it was just over eleven weeks until Gordie returned from Montana.

The two of them could manage. Right?

He turned back to Manny. The younger man's dark eyes regarded him with curiosity.

"I also finished the oil and filter change for Mrs. Spagnoletti before you clocked in this morning."

That was another thing. These days, his mornings started late thanks to midmorning school runs and bakery drop-offs. Miss Marie had offered to help yesterday, but Hank was still logging late-night hours trying to stay on top of the garage backlog.

Regardless, he'd been working well into the early morning hours, trying to make up for lost time at the shop. His reasoning was twofold. First, the backlog of vehicles needing repair seemed to grow by the day. Second—and maybe the heavier of the two—was that the more time he spent away from the ranch, the easier it was to avoid the tangle of emotions stirred up by having Olive and her children underfoot—not to mention the big goofy dog. He snorted, picturing the Lab's most recent toilet paper crime scene.

He grinned at his right-hand mechanic. "Thanks, Manny. You're a lifesaver." When his cell phone buzzed with an incoming call, he held up an index finger; he still wanted to ask if he was willing to pull overtime. That way Hank could take Olive and the kids to dinner at the bed and breakfast.

Rocking back on his heels, he shook his head. As he put the call on speaker, he tried to wrap his mind around how much his life had flipped in under a week.

"Hank & Gordie's Garage, Hank speaking."

"Big Country, just the man I needed to speak with." Mrs. Spagnoletti's singsong trill carried through the shop.

"Good morning, Mrs. S. And yes, your car is ready and waiting." He winked at Manny, who fidgeted with the slip of paper in his hand.

"Wonderful, I'll find someone to drop me off later this morning since I already have a million and one errands to run for this year's spring carnival."

After reciting the amount due, he ended the call. "That woman... Always donating her time and efforts to one worthy cause or another."

When Manny averted his eyes, a niggle of dread appeared out of thin air to crawl up Hank's spine.

"It's true, Mr. and Mrs. S. have always worked hard to make amends for their nephew's bad business practices."

Manny's tone didn't quite match the casual words, prompting Hank to tug at his beard as a passing motorist caught his eye. Outside, snow flurried down from a dreary, slate-gray sky.

He quickly issued a silent prayer there'd be no repeat of the recent blizzard—not with the garage bays near capacity—before returning his gaze to the man in front of him.

Picking up the thread of conversation, he pictured the notorious Aaron Parker, the dirty developer behind the scandal that had rocked the small town. "Hard to believe Doc Wells had been married to that crook before she took over the vet position."

"Ms. Emerson is a very nice lady." Manny's eyes flicked to the clock hanging next to the calendar. "Mr. Valentine—"

At the timbre of his employee's voice and the use of Hank's surname, dread curled around his rib cage. "We've got a lot on our plates today. What's on your mind, Manny?"

His mechanic shifted his weight and looked at Hank. "I just got offered a lead mechanic position at a busy shop in Phoenix. Better pay, benefits—the whole package. It's an opportunity I can't pass up."

Hank nodded slowly, tugging at his beard. "I get it, Manny. Just wish the timing was better."

Manny gave a small, apologetic smile. "Me too. But my wife is expecting our fourth child, and this is a chance to move up. I hope you understand."

Hank's vision blurred. He couldn't have heard Manny right— not with Gordie out of commission for the next three months. He mentally tallied what they might manage before Manny packed up his tools and headed south—jobs piling up, deadlines looming, and no time to find help.

But the look he gave Hank answered the question better than words ever could.

Two weeks' notice would've helped. Instead, Hank signed the check to cover Manny's pay through the month's end, clapped him on the back, and wished him Godspeed.

All that remained was the heavy coil of dread dropping like a lump of coal straight into his gut. *Lord, remember my petitions for a clone?*

He had no time to waste wallowing over the departure. After all, family was priority, and his best mechanic was expected at the new shop for orientation that afternoon. But first his cousin, now his top man…and then the surprise addition of houseguests?

With no time to waste, Hank handled a few phone calls, turned over the keys to Mrs. Spagnoletti's vehicle, and replaced the battery in the pickup that Charles Bloom used to transport floral arrangements. Then he sat down to wrestle with an ad for the town newspaper.

If part-time reporter Kate Wells was at that evening's dinner party, he might be able to fast-track finding Manny's replacement.

After shredding his third effort to craft the job posting, he chucked it into the waste basket beneath the counter when the bell above the door chimed. He lifted his head, breath catching at the sight of Olive, a swirl of snowflakes trailing behind her.

Since he'd refused her offer of help in the garage the previous evening, the air between them had cooled.

She stomped her boots on the entry mat and lifted her eyes. "Wow, it's really starting to come down out there."

When she pulled the beanie off her head, letting those caramel-colored waves fall around her rosy cheeks, thoughts of his staffing problems slipped out of his mind.

"How did you, uh…" He stepped around the counter and nodded toward the window as he reached for his beard.

A brief smile flickered across her face. "Annie let me deliver a few catering orders, so I thought I'd stop by to check on the status of my car."

As if out of habit, she placed a hand on her abdomen. Had it grown rounder since he dropped her off at the bakery that morning?

At the mention of her vehicle, concerns about Manny's sudden departure resurfaced—along with the growing backlog of work he couldn't possibly clear before spring, at least, not with this latest setback.

He groaned. "About that—"

The doorbell jingled again, and their heads turned in unison.

"Hey, you two, how's it goin'?"

Swiping at his salt-and-pepper goatee, Councilman Persh strode to the front of the store and clasped Hank's outstretched hand, then glanced from one to the other as if he sensed the underlying tension.

"Did I interrupt something?"

Olive swallowed. "No, Mr. Persh—pardon me, Persh… I was asking Hank about my vehicle."

She side-eyed him, and he could read the question lingering within her golden gaze.

Persh's eyebrows furrowed. "Oh yeah, bummer about Man—"

Panic ratcheted Hank's pulse. "What can I do for you, Councilman?" He willed his friend to refrain from spilling the beans about his mechanic's resignation, while feeling Olive's weighty stare. Having already turned down her offer of help, no way he wanted her knowing he was in deep water now.

How had news even traveled that fast?

Persh pinned him with a confused expression before schooling his features. "My bride asked me to stop by and pick up a mesh thingy for holding kids' toys." He snapped his fingers. "And to remind you about tonight's dinner."

Hank bit back a decline to the invitation. "Right, we just received a new supply of seat organizers…which should be over there." He pointed at a display rack containing a variety of auto accessories.

"You were saying?"

Once Persh had slipped into the vehicle supply aisle, Olive had wasted no time cornering him about her car, and he snapped.

Again.

"This isn't a good time."

His words came out sharper than he meant, and regret hit fast as a flicker of hurt crossed her pretty face.

She took a step back. "Oh… I see. Okay, then." Starting for the door, she paused. "I'll just wait until you pick me up later."

In that split second, he couldn't remember the last time he'd felt like a bigger, meaner grizzly bear of a bonehead.

Her coat tails flapped behind her as she strode away.

He'd messed up. When was he going to get it right?

Before he could call after her, Persh stepped into her path.

Holding the toy bag in one hand, the councilman smiled. "Looking forward to hosting you and your kiddos tonight."

Olive's shoulders rose with her breath, then settled into place as she returned his smile. "Me too," she said, pressing a palm against the door. "Annie mentioned it's casual?"

Persh nodded. "You bet—nothing formal about us folks."

He let out his usual guffaw as she swept out, leaving behind a frostiness that matched the icy glare she'd leveled at Hank.

"Please let her know I'll bring a dish to share."

And before the councilman could respond, the door closed behind her. "What was that all about?"

The man he'd known for most of his life approached the counter, his purchase tucked under one arm and a number eleven forming between his eyebrows.

Hank smoothed a palm over his head. "Let's just say I'm not winning friends and influencing people this morning."

After wrapping up Persh's transaction and confirming his attendance at the inn that evening, Hank divided his time between garage bays for the next few hours. When he stopped for a short break and checked the time, his pulse tripled.

Even if he left the shop right then, he'd be late to pick up Olive and the kids.

He placed a quick call to Miss Marie and arranged alternate transportation, throwing in a promise that her next oil change was on the house.

"And please tell Olive I'll be at the ranch by six o'clock to take them to the B and B."

He only hoped he could keep his promise. Because every time it seemed he was making headway on inventory, another vehicle rolled onto the lot—making it impossible to work on Olive's SUV until he'd honored his other commitments.

By midafternoon, just when he was about to cut out early, a tow call came in clear across town.

These things I have spoken unto you, that in me ye might have peace. In the world ye shall have tribulation: but be of good cheer; I have overcome the world.

The verse spilled into his spirit as he secured the broken-down pickup and waited for his customer's ride to arrive. Based on personal experience, he knew that followers of Jesus were not exempt from trouble.

Still, he hoped the old wives' tale about bad things happening in threes would hold. With his cousin out of commission, his unexpected lodgers, and now Manny, he ought to be in the clear.

Once back at the shop, he slid beneath a newer sedan, slipping easily into the role that had felt like second nature since he and Gordie opened the place after Hank had graduated high school. Fixing things had always been his superpower—the one thing he excelled at.

But relationships? He snorted. His failed engagement served as proof that his own heart was beyond repair.

There was no guessing where his mind was headed—visions of Olive and her family kept creeping in. Honestly, thoughts of her were never far off, especially after her surprise visit to the garage that morning, the scent of yeast and spices still clinging to her coat when he'd brusquely sent her on her way.

He'd make it up to her that evening—his behavior and missing her family's afternoon pickup. After apologizing, he'd explain everything to her when the time was right.

But when he finally poked his head out from under the hood of a newfangled sports car, he registered the darkening sky beyond the windows.

Oh no. Please don't be after five thirty.

After grabbing the towel stuffed in his back pocket, he wiped off his greasy hands. But one look at his cell phone and he groaned.

He then released the hood, its echo reverberating off the cement walls. Punching in Olive's cell phone number, he raced from the bay toward his closet-sized space in the back of the shop.

"I'm sorry to have missed you. Please leave a message after the tone." Her soft voice brought back the hurt he'd seen in her eyes, and his heart clenched.

Shedding his work clothes, he waited for the sound of the beep before blurting out an apology and relaying his ETA.

Despite the less-than-ideal weather conditions, weekend traffic was also congested, which delayed his commute by several minutes. Once his truck crunched over the snowpack that paved the winding driveway, it was well past seven o'clock.

"That's odd." He pinched his eyebrows.

From the exterior, no lights shone from inside the ranch house. Yet it was too early for Olive and the kids to be in bed.

After throwing his vehicle into Park and cutting the engine, he shot out of the cab and into the mudroom. The rattling of Roman's tags hanging from his collar preceded the big dog's arrival. His tail wagged at the sight of Hank.

Absently, he bent to rub the Lab's large head as he pulled off his boots, then peered down the dark hallway. "Olive? Simon? Holly?"

His voice echoed back, and an unreasonable panic zinged through his veins. He scoffed at himself.

What's the worst that could've happened?

Without waiting for an answer, he flipped on the lights—Roman glued to his leg—as he scanned the kitchen and great room before heading straight for the guest room. The guest bath door was shut—a habit to keep the dog out of the toilet paper—but no light spilled from beneath it.

At the end of the hall, he knocked on the closed door of the room Olive shared with her kids.

No answer. He tugged at his beard, fingers brushing the short hair at his temple, then returned to the kitchen, where the white edge of a slip of paper caught beneath a chair leg grabbed his attention.

As he stooped to retrieve a note written in Olive's scrawl, Roman pushed against him.

He read aloud. "'Found alternate transportation, O.'"

Realizing he'd just struck out for the third time that day— first by snapping at Olive in the garage, then by missing their pickup—he tried to stifle his guilt as his plan to sell the ranch resurfaced. He'd even contacted a realtor, his hopes pinned on funding an expanded garage and a full crew.

But ever since the Harts arrived, he'd had second thoughts.

Still, after the day he'd had, the urge to sell felt stronger than ever. Rosie's accident had been the catalyst—driving away potential partners, including a fiancée, and cementing his belief that he wasn't worthy of love.

Legend or no legend.

Roman barked once, sharp and knowing.

Hank sighed. "Yeah, I know. I'm the one in the doghouse tonight."

Olive released the plasticware she clutched as Lacey Sweetwater Pershing took it from her gloved hand.

Lacey was one of several kindhearted parishioners who'd delivered meals, groceries, and toys—and even a few clothes—to the ranch house after Sunday service.

A flush rose to her cheeks.

At first, their kindness made her uneasy. But her plan to avoid attachment unraveled the moment everyone pitched in—despite her refusals.

Even Pastor Mark had quietly dipped into the church's benevolent fund to cover Simon and Holly's tuition at the church-run preschool-through-second-grade program—a gesture that still made her heart squeeze with gratitude.

"I hope my husband told you this wasn't necessary." Lacey brandished the container while she batted an errant copper-colored curl with her free hand.

Olive grimaced. "I'm afraid I didn't let the councilman get a word in edgewise, but it's really nothing." Following a midafternoon detour to the grocery store with Miss Marie, she'd picked up the ingredients for a simple salad.

"Well, it looks wonderful," Lacey said.

Small fingers tugged on Olive's coat, and her eyes dropped

to Holly. Her daughter pointed at a dome glass cover revealing a plate piled with cookies. Simon stood next to it, bobbing in place, eyes hungry.

She shook her head and lowered her voice. "I imagine those are for the inn's guests."

Lacey scooted next to her and bent down to the children's level.

"If your momma says it's okay, you may each have one to tide you over until dinner."

When Lacey straightened, three pairs of eyes sought out Olive's, and she giggled. "How can I say no, now?"

While the other woman lifted the lid and the kids picked out their respective treats, Olive's gaze shifted to the charming living room. Furnished with a floral sofa that flanked a wood-burning fireplace—flames dancing in the hearth—it flowed toward a staircase at the far end of the room. Annie had mentioned that the second floor in the B and B accommodated the owner's suite and a small nursery.

To her right, a well-appointed dining area was arranged with a few high-top mahogany tables, an antique hutch against the back wall, and a long rectangular table. The view from this room overlooked a wooden deck at the front of the inn.

Each table was topped with place settings and etched glassware. Simple bud vase centerpieces displayed red roses and baby's breath.

A nervous chuckle slipped from Olive's lips, and she waved a hand toward the empty chairs. "Please don't tell me we're the first ones here."

Lacey's long skirt swished against her legs as she scurried toward the swinging doors identical to those at the bakery.

"Follow me." She winked, then pushed into the kitchen with Olive and her children at her heels. "Since the snow stopped, Persh fired up the propane heaters. And everyone's on the back deck." She nodded toward a short hallway, a door at the end.

"Momma, can we?" Cheeks sprinkled with crumbs, Holly jiggled in place.

"Yeah, Mom, is it okay?" Simon's eyes, much like her own, shone with eagerness.

She shooed them past the large center island covered in mouth-watering dishes. As they took off running, her heart pinched with quiet relief at how easily they both had settled into this new life.

If only that were true for me.

Bruised from Hank's earlier brush-off that morning and the previous evening, she'd almost called Lacey with an excuse to avoid the dinner party, especially when Miss Marie had shown up at the bakery in place of the mechanic. Still, the older woman had assured her Hank would pick them up at the ranch as planned. And the children had done nothing but talk nonstop about getting to play with Josie, the Wellses' seven-year-old, and an older brother recently adopted into their growing family.

But when the microwave's clock had changed from six to six thirty with no word from Hank, she'd punched in Lacey's number on her cell phone to extend her regrets. That's when the woman told Olive to sit tight because their driver was on the way.

Rather than Hank, however, Kate Wells—Jack's half-sister—arrived twenty minutes later. After scribbling a quick note for their family's host, Olive ushered her children into the back seat of the woman's vehicle, and in less than half an hour, they'd been dropped off in front of the historic inn.

Stepping into the B and B's warmth, the scent of fresh-baked pastries—sweet like the town bakery, laced with something savory—had enveloped her like a cozy sweater.

"Everything smells divine… How can I help?"

Lacey tsked, her emerald-green gaze meeting hers. The freckles dusting her nose reminded her of a smattering of cinnamon.

"You're our guests! Plus, you've already done more than enough." She set the salad container on the counter next to the assorted platters and pried off the lid. Plump sliced strawberries, crumbled feta cheese, and toasted almonds topped a bed of fresh spinach—lightly tossed with strawberry vinaigrette.

It fit in perfectly with the post-Valentine's Day decor displayed throughout the inn.

"Why don't you join the others on the deck, and I'll be out shortly?"

When Olive hesitated, Lacey offered a soft smile. "I insist."

It would've been the ideal time for Olive to inquire about accommodations for her and the kids, especially since Annie had shared the most recent news about the furnace that morning. Not only did it need repair, but they'd shut off the water to eliminate the possibility that the old pipes might freeze and burst.

But before she could bring it up, the door at the end of the hallway swung open and Persh strode into view. He pressed a quick kiss to his wife's cheek—a tender gesture that made Olive's heart clench with the weight of her losses—then turned to her.

"I thought my wife might've put you to work." He guffawed, then sidestepped to avoid Lacey's swat with a potholder.

"I was just telling her to head out back." The woman glided toward an ultramodern oven and lowered the door to peer inside.

Persh sidled past Olive and poked his head between the swinging doors. Swiping at his goatee, he faced Olive with questioning eyes. "Did Big Country drop you off?"

At the mention of Hank, she recalled the voicemail she'd listened to after she and the kids had piled out of Kate's vehicle. Despite his apology, his behavior had stirred up memories of promises made—and broken—throughout her life. But once she moved out of the ranch house and into the inn, with her car back in working order, she'd no longer be his concern.

"Kate picked up Olive and the kids."

Lacey answered for her with a look she leveled at her husband, the kind that spoke volumes without a single word. He gave a quiet nod, clearly reading between the lines.

Just look at the trouble we've already caused.

Not wishing to draw additional attention to their situation,

Olive pasted on a smile and moved toward the hallway. "I'd better check on Simon and Holly."

So many faces. That had been her first thought, though many she recognized. Several of the ladies had dropped by the ranch on Sunday, and a couple of other townsfolk had popped into the bakery during the week—including Mr. Timmons, the owner of Twice-Loved Treasures, the secondhand shop.

The number of bodies and the warmth from the portable heaters on the raised patio created a cozy ambiance. Moving off to the side, Olive took a moment to take everything in.

Two large folding tables held appetizers, beverages, and Valentine-themed paper plates, cups, and napkins. The glittering stars overhead—and the miniature twinkle lights draped from the branches throughout the grounds—provided enough illumination to pick out Simon and Holly playing in the snow with the Pershings' toddler daughter, Ada Mae. She also recognized the Rogerses' son, and Jack and Emerson's girl, Josie.

"I'm so glad you made it, Olive."

Miss Marie's voice startled her at first, but Olive relaxed as the woman pulled her into a quick, motherly hug—one that caught her off guard with its warmth and made her ache a little, since her own mother had rarely offered affection, much less comfort. Then Miss Marie indicated the distinguished older gentleman at her side.

"I'm Charles Bloom… It's a pleasure to meet you, Ms. Hart." He extended his hand, eyes sparkling with kindness.

Olive returned the greeting, recalling Annie's mention of the couple's years-long courtship, followed by a quiet ceremony witnessed by the Pershings.

"I'm guessing your shop supplied the stunning floral centerpieces this evening."

The man beamed as he slipped an arm around Miss Marie's shoulders. "You'd be guessing right, and I'm glad you like them."

Following Miss Marie and Charles's lead, the remaining adults welcomed her to Sweetwater, each asking questions about her plans. Since she still hadn't decided to plant roots in the small town after the birth of her baby, she kept her answers vague.

Soon, Lacey emerged from the inn to gather everyone, and Pastor Mark—who'd followed Kate in from the overflow parking—offered a prayer over the food and the evening's fellowship.

When she lifted her head, she spotted Hank walking along the same path, his gaze sweeping the crowd as the remaining guests moved indoors from the patio.

As coincidence would have it, their place settings were side by side at one of the high-top tables reserved for the adults. The children sat at the long dining table with Carley, the young woman who worked part-time at the bakery and assisted Emerson at the wildlife preserve. Carley had graciously offered to sit with the toddlers and run interference if needed.

Persh directed the flow of traffic between the dining area and the kitchen, where homemade lasagna, dinner rolls, and assorted side dishes were arranged buffet style the length of the butcher-block counter.

"Can I refill anyone's drink?" their hostess asked, scurrying behind the chairs with a pitcher of iced water in her hand. She stopped beside Olive and topped off her glass.

She'd tasted the sweet beverage Lacey had brought to the ranch that weekend and remembered to ask Annie about it. Something about a century-old legend: couples falling in love thanks to Constance Sweetwater, the town's founder, and the tradition continuing with Gram and Pop Sweetwater passing the responsibility down to their granddaughter, with one stipulation: to maintain it through fervent prayers and matchmaking intervention.

Next to her, Hank covered his glass with a large hand and cleared his throat. "I'm good, thanks."

The man had apologized a second time when they'd discovered their place cards side by side in the center of their plates—before being swept up in chitchat at the table.

While Olive had been half-focused on Simon and Holly laughing at the next table over, Kate excused herself mid-meal to take a call. A few moments later, Hank pushed back his chair and followed her through the swinging café doors into the kitchen.

"Have you spilled the news about the film crew booked at the inn for the next two months?" Persh's voice rose above the chatter, pulling her back to her table's conversation.

Lord, no—that can't be. She'd counted on moving her and the children out of the ranch house and into one of the cottages. Especially since Hank refused her offer to help at the garage. Suddenly, the room felt stifling, and she feared she might pass out at the table.

"Pardon me." She slid her chair back, the legs scraping against the floorboards. Plucking the cloth napkin from her lap, she tossed it onto her half-eaten meal. As she stood, she noticed the concern in the fire chief's eyes, his stubbled jaw clenched tight.

But without missing a beat, she hurried to the nearest exit and stepped onto the front porch. Sconces flanked either side of the door, their warm glow complementing the string lights woven through dormant ivy climbing the trellis at the walkway's start.

Without the propane heaters' warmth, the chilly air was a sharp contrast to the cozy back patio and the inn's interior, and she gasped at the sudden cold. Within seconds, she caught voices drifting from the far side of the deck, where a walkway led down to the backyard.

"What did Olive say when you told her?"

Her eyes adjusted to the dim light just enough to make out Hank and Kate standing in the shadows. Without thinking, she stepped across the wooden planks and stopped at the railing.

"Told Olive what?"

Their heads snapped toward her, the surprise in Hank's pale blue eyes unmistakable even in the shadows.

"I'll head back inside and leave you both to it." Kate patted him on the shoulder before disappearing down the cement staircase.

Olive's teeth chattered as Hank shoved his hands into the front pockets of his denim jeans and rounded the picket fence to climb the deck stairs. After pulling off the scarf he'd likely grabbed during his detour through the kitchen, he draped it gently around her neck.

His woodsy scent, mingled with the sharp tang of fresh oil, stirred warm memories of working alongside Granddad as a teenager—and made her heart beat a little faster.

But whether it was thoughts of her grandfather—or the larger-than-life man before her who stirred the flutter in her belly and left her momentarily speechless—she couldn't tell.

Hank opened and closed his mouth, as if unsure where to begin.

"Manny—my best mechanic—resigned this morning."

"Huh?" Olive blinked up at him. "I thought Manny was full-time?"

"He was. But his wife's due any day now, and when a better offer came in from the Valley—more hours, better pay—he jumped. Can't blame him, but the timing stinks."

The hits just kept coming. She gripped the railing tighter, fighting to keep from unraveling in front of him.

A puff of breath lingered between them, a closeness Olive refused to acknowledge. But the weight of his words nearly buckled her knees—especially with his business partner already on medical leave for the next three months.

He ran a hand through his short-cropped copper hair, the glow of the nearby lights catching the strands.

"And my backlog of work just keeps growing. Even though the parts for your car should arrive tomorrow—"

The screen door slammed against its hinges behind the constable, who crossed the deck and approached without invitation.

"If you want to know what I think—"

Am I the last to hear this news?

She needed to get back inside to check on the kids, but was finally on the verge of answers.

"Jack." Hank's tone sharpened with an edge.

The other man pushed his Stetson—a cover for a head of

strawberry-blonde curls—higher on his forehead, then raised both palms in front of his chest.

"Hey, wasn't it Olive who said she knows her way around a car engine?"

Hank must've shared her offer with the constable.

A coyote's howl split the quiet, sharp as her nerves.

She cradled her belly, eyes lifting to the stars. They reminded her of the lullabies she used to sing—back when life had felt more certain.

The baby inside her kicked, and her gaze snapped to Hank. His shuttered expression confirmed her suspicions.

With Jack on her side, maybe Hank wouldn't be so quick to veto the idea. And besides being a way to repay the mechanic's hospitality, helping out at the garage part-time might ease the strain when it came time to settle the bill.

She touched his arm. "You need help. And I'm offering. Please, Hank."

His shoulders sagged. "You really think you can manage all that?"

"You think I can't?"

His lips twitched. "All right, then, Miss Olive Sunshine. Let's give it a shot—but only until your car is fixed."

Her breath hitched. For once, she wasn't just the one in need—she was needed. And maybe, just maybe, that counted for something.

The thought flickered—just a start, nothing more. Yet if she proved herself, who could say where it might lead?

But as she met his unreadable gaze, she couldn't help but wonder—at what cost to her heart?

Chapter Four

Flat on his back, Hank swiped his knuckles across his forehead. He ground his heels into the floor, and the dolly slid from underneath a classic T-Bird.

He was fixing the old girl for Mr. Timmons to sell at his shop. Once parked in front of Twice-Loved Treasures on Main Street, it was sure to draw attention and bring in new customers.

An influx of which Hank didn't need at the moment.

He hoisted himself off the wooden roller and kicked it aside. Jamming his fists into the small of his back, he stretched out the kinks.

The low lighting and dark sky outside the bay windows could've passed for dusk, though it was barely morning.

After last night's dinner party dispersed, he'd dropped off Olive and the kids at the ranch with little fanfare. He'd pulled an all-nighter at the garage—broken up by a few short breaks to refill his cup with the always-ready strong brew.

He meandered to the silent lobby but didn't flip on the overhead fixtures. Sunlight bounced off the snow piled along the curb and through the front window, providing just enough illumination to find the coffee maker. His thoughts drifted to the previous day, beginning with Manny's sudden resignation and ending with a truce of sorts with Olive.

He shook his head with a grunt.

But only after he accepted her cockamamie offer.

He rolled his eyes. The Lord worked in mysterious ways—no doubt about it.

But the rest of the evening had gone off without a hitch. Once the ladies had finished clearing the kitchen, Olive found her kids on the sofa where Josie read from her *Coco the Chimpanzee* adventure book. Amidst the kids' sleepy protests, they'd said their goodbyes.

And now, as he slugged down the bitter brew, his gaze flicked to the brightening horizon.

I don't know what it is about that woman, Lord.

One moment, her stubbornness matched his. In the next, she practiced quiet patience with her children. Not to mention a strong work ethic that he admired.

But she always seemed to be on guard, as if she tread on pins and needles.

He left his mug beside the half-empty carafe, then tugged on his beard. That watchful tension she carried—like she was always braced for something—probably explained why a pregnant woman with two kids and a dog had braved a blizzard to show up in Sweetwater.

But he'd never dig into her reasons, assuming they were connected to the nonprofit Annie worked with that supported expectant mothers.

At the counter, he checked the open work tickets for the day. He had a small window to hole up in the back room and eke in a few minutes of shut-eye before opening for business.

Last he heard, the weather forecast called for milder temps with no precipitation, which lessened the chance of receiving a callout for tows.

He raised his eyes skyward, a prayer of gratitude on his lips, then moved toward his home away from home in the rear of the garage.

Patchwork blanket in hand, he dropped onto the mattress and pulled it up to his beard. He pictured his mother working on the quilt when he and Rosie were kids, but fell asleep dogged by images of almond-shaped eyes and caramel-colored waves. And the faint memory of a floral scent like the gardens once flourishing on the ranch.

Barely thirty minutes later, Hank surfaced from a fitful sleep, unrested and still dog-tired, but duty waited. After he flipped on the lights in the lobby and unlocked the front door, his cell phone chimed as if on cue.

"Good morning, Hank & Gordie's Garage—oh, hello, Mrs. Greer."

The older woman, a recent widow and long-time resident, had been trying to handle the routine tasks her late husband had taken care of. And all on top of her job at the Town Square offices.

"Okay, slow down, Maggie—yes, just bring it by this afternoon and I'll take a look."

He entered a note into his software system to investigate a strange knocking noise in the woman's engine at no charge.

The doorbell dinged, and Hank lifted his gaze to the front windows. The fire chief bent low to enter the doorway. Finn giggled and waved at Hank from his perch on his father's shoulders, a croissant clutched in a mitten.

"Hey, there's the man of the hour!" Josh wiped his boots on the floor mat, then grasped the boy under his arms and set him on the floor.

Finn pulled off his stocking cap and took off running toward a bin full of toys Hank had added to the lobby.

Rounding the counter, Hank met Josh halfway and grasped his hand for a quick shake.

"What can I do for you, Chief?" A glance toward the street revealed his friend's fire-engine-red SUV parked at the curb. "Everything okay with your ride?"

Josh nodded. "Affirmative. But I still believe that Annie's catering van must've come with multiple lives like her rescue cat." He palmed the back of his neck and chuckled.

Hank laughed while picturing the rickety van the baker used to deliver her goodies. "Then what do I owe the pleasure?"

Had his friend sensed the tension between him and Olive the previous night?

Was this a simple welfare check?

Josh glanced around the shop, taking in the cluttered workstation and half-drained coffeepot.

"I know you're buried in cars needing repair…and until you replace Manny—"

"Daddy, wook." Out of breath, Finn brandished a Matchbox hook and ladder with his free hand.

Josh ruffled the boy's dark hair that favored his, though his late foster brother was Finn's biological father.

"You're right, buddy, that's just like the one I drive."

The chief's son beamed, then toddled back across the lobby.

Josh's comment reminded him that he was running the shop alone—that is, until he and Olive worked out a schedule and Kate posted his want ad in the paper and online outlets.

"What do you need, Chief?"

A smile edged across his friend's face. "It's a favor for Annie."

Now, that was a different story.

He'd never been able to turn down the person who kept him stocked with his favorite treats.

Just the thought of her signature lemon bars, and his mouth watered.

Hank snorted. "Her van needs a tune-up after all?"

Josh shook his head. "No, but the repairman is giving her the runaround and…" Finn rejoined them, raised his arms, and his dad scooped him against his chest. "Since she promised the apartment to Olive, she feels terrible about how long it's taking to repair the furnace."

Therein lay Hank's dilemma. He should've felt relieved to move Olive and her kids out of his house. Instead, it left a hollow ache he hadn't expected.

He swallowed. Wasn't that what he wanted? To focus on the business, not on fixing their problems?

But it would get Olive and the kids a step closer to independence. And wasn't that what they deserved?

"Can you swing it?"

Josh shifted Finn from arm to arm while waiting for Hank's answer.

Olive had the day off, and it was the weekend, so no need to pick up the kids. He peered at the clock over his shoulder, then clapped the fire chief on his back.

"Tell Annie I'll be there."

A little after one o'clock, Hank steered his tow truck onto the gravel drive behind the bakery. He pulled up next to the catering van that had seen better days, yet still got the job done.

Seems we share something in common.

Grabbing a toolbox from the back seat, he snickered and hiked up the walkway to the back entrance.

Stepping into the empty kitchen, warmth enveloped him. He savored the aroma of fresh-baked bread for a split second, then scooted into a back room. Mechanical equipment lined the compact space, where he located the unit that heated the upstairs apartment.

Crouching before the furnace, he muttered as he inspected the wiring and pipes. "Jumpin' jack fish—needs more than a new part..." His gaze caught a scattering of fine sawdust along the edge of the panel. A critter? Could be. Vandals? Hopefully not again.

Not fifteen minutes later, he reentered the kitchen and almost plowed into one of Annie's employees.

He opened his mouth to apologize—

Then his breath hitched.

Of course, it was her. Almond eyes, caramel waves, that same guarded wariness just beneath the polite expression.

He hadn't expected to see her here, which made zero sense, considering she was practically everywhere he turned these days.

"Olive, I—I'm so sorry." He might as well tattoo that phrase across his forehead.

Faint shadows clung beneath her eyes, making her look even more worn down than she had yesterday.

His gut clenched. The news about the furnace would only add to the fine lines etched into her forehead.

One hand instinctively braced her belly, a nervous chuckle escaping her lips.

"Hank! What are you doing here?" Her gaze landed on the toolbox he carried. "Oh—"

"I was going to ask the same thing." He scuffed a boot against the tile and tugged on his beard.

Olive turned and placed an insulated bag on the counter behind her. "Annie needed help, and the kids were bored. So when Lacey offered to babysit, Persh swung by and picked us up."

"Should I pick everyone up later today?" The offer slipped out before he could stop it. But with her car still out of commission— and his conscience riding him—he couldn't help himself.

She pressed her palms into the small of her back and arched into them. Gnawing on her bottom lip, she peered at him through thick lashes.

"If it's no bother," she said, though her tone sounded like she expected it to be.

What was with her aversion to accepting help from others? Especially when she had no problem returning the favor.

"We should probably talk about your schedule at the shop, too." He still didn't know how he felt about that. But he was in a bind.

"I'll be here."

He recalled his broken promises from the previous day and dropped his gaze. That's when Annie bustled in from the bakery floor, her hands already in motion.

"Oh, hi, Big Country." She smiled, then blew at a strand of hair that escaped from her messy bun. "Figure out the problem with the furnace, I hope?"

Eagerness radiated from her eyes as she adjusted the black

frames on the bridge of her nose, while Olive's gaze held a quiet wariness, like she was bracing for bad news.

He cleared the gravel from his throat. "I hate to be the bad guy, but something is fishy, and the whole unit needs to be replaced."

No need to bring up his concerns about a repeat of the strange shenanigans that occurred at the bakery last year.

If anything, he'd mention it to Josh the next time he ran into him.

Annie groaned. "Ugh. I'm not surprised." She peeked at Olive, her skin pale. "Please tell me everything went okay with the next-door delivery."

"Oh, yes, Rick was…" Olive paused, choosing her words. "Accommodating."

The previous year, Annie had problems with her neighbor. The sporting goods store owner had tried a scare tactic to force her into selling the prime space behind the bakery that now featured her thriving Parisian-inspired café.

Annie rolled her eyes, then swiped her palms across her apron. "Well, he should be. He did agree to sell my health food items to make restitution for his bad sportsmanship."

She addressed Olive with a critical eye. "Honey, please take a break—you're making me tired."

Winking, she gave Olive a gentle push in Hank's direction. "And thanks for looking at the furnace."

Annie busied herself at the sink. But Hank stopped paying attention as soon as Olive touched his forearm. The fluttering softness reminded him of a butterfly wing—delicate and fleeting, just like the ones that hovered around his mom's flowering shrubs in the spring.

"Do you have a minute, before we pick up the kids?"

The clock above the café doors said no, but her smooth, warm palm said otherwise.

He coughed. Tilting his head toward the bakery, he led her through the café doors.

Pink and black decor—reminiscent of an old-time bakery outfitted with a classic soda fountain at the end of a long counter—invited visitors to linger. The sweet scents sealed the deal.

Without warning, he longed to do exactly that—to linger. Not just in the cozy bakery, but with the woman across from him. They'd chosen the same table where she'd passed out just a week earlier—seven days since the Harts had upended his solitary life.

"Can I get you something to eat or drink?"

Olive began to rise, but he held up a hand.

"Your boss told you to take a break, remember?" He screwed up his mouth, hoping to earn one of her dazzling smiles.

Her throat bobbed as if she were swallowing her nerves.

"Hank, I—"

"Olive, please—"

They spoke over each other. He lifted a hand, palm up. "Ladies first."

That earned him a tiny grin and a win in his book.

"I hate to be a burden—"

He opened his mouth, but she stopped him with the same look he'd seen her level on her kids when they misbehaved.

"As you probably figured out, my family needs a place to stay a bit longer—"

She licked her lips—a mouth he had no business noticing—then brushed a hand over her ponytail. At first glance, she looked young, but exhaustion clutched her like an extra layer.

He was too old—and too worn down himself—to be getting any ideas. Wasn't he?

"So the sooner I can start work at the garage—" she took a deep breath, then exhaled "—the sooner I can pay our way."

Even after accepting her offer, second thoughts had lingered.

"Look, Olive, you're—"

She didn't miss the flicker in his eyes toward her ample middle.

The gold flecks that peppered her irises sparked like embers on a campfire.

"I'm what…pregnant?" Humor laced her tone.

He shrugged. "Well—yeah."

Her bottom lip jutted out. Way too full, if you asked him.

Her palm rubbed her belly in slow circles.

"I've already cleared it with Annie. And I saw my new doctor two days ago—"

He inhaled the savory fragrances that flooded the space. His breath released in a *whoosh*. She knew he needed her help because the sooner they thinned out the backlog, the sooner her car would be in business.

And that would free him up from chauffeur duty. But had it really been that bad?

Olive squared her shoulders and sat a little taller on her chair. "I'm starting on Monday."

Hadn't he asked the Lord to clone him? He rolled his eyes.

I guess He showed me.

What in the Sam Hill am I doing?

The old phrase made Olive think of her granddad, his memory softening her nerves as she faced her reflection in the garage's public restroom.

She smoothed her palms across the oversized khaki coveralls Hank had tossed at her when they'd arrived at dark thirty—a term she'd heard Annie use.

A grimace creased her forehead. The circus-tent-sized uniform might be a joke, but she wasn't laughing. Still, she hadn't backed down from a challenge yet.

And her initial visit to the garage had reminded her of happier times as a teenager. Days that had been filled with grease-streaked joy and Granddad's steady encouragement. Something her ex-husband would never have understood—or supported if it meant working outside of their home.

"You okay in there?"

Hank's voice carried from the other side of the door, his tone concerned.

She couldn't stop the flicker of a smile. "Be out in a few minutes."

As she pulled her hair into a topknot identical to Annie's signature style, she tucked away the memories and yawned.

This stint might stretch her thin, but when Hank admitted his mechanic had left him in a bind, he hadn't exactly turned her down when she offered again. Pinning down a start date had been the tricky part.

"Hold your horses, little one," she whispered with a giggle, a familiar flutter answering back. "Momma's got this."

She reported for duty in the waiting room and spotted Roman curled up on the floor by the counter. The kids had slept over at the B and B the previous night, and Hank had insisted she bring the dog that morning.

Pale blue eyes gleamed with suppressed laughter as they raked over her.

Hands on her hips, Olive raised a brow, trying and failing to suppress a grin. "Something funny you care to share, mister?"

Hank clamped his mouth closed. "No, ma'am."

She flicked her wrist toward the door to the garage floor. "Okay then, what's first on the agenda—boss?"

"Pull up a chair." Hank indicated a tall chair with wheels in front of the computer. And for the next hour, he gave her an overview of the accounting software, then disappeared into the shop.

Her heart sank. The hands on the clock seemed frozen in place. She'd never been one for sitting still when there was real work to be done.

Was it too much to ask to pick apart an engine?

Her gaze drifted longingly to the door, half expecting the scent of grease and metal to seep through and call her name.

After she entered the final invoice from the first pile into the system, she pressed her fist into her lower back.

"How're you holding up?"

She jerked, and Roman barked as Hank sauntered into the lobby.

"When will you let me work back there?" she asked, sharper

than she meant. But she didn't take it back—she wasn't here to be humored.

The telltale tug of his coppery beard confirmed what she suspected—he was stalling. The motion drew her gaze, and her pulse skipped.

Paul Bunyan—the name her son used that first night.

He grunted. "You wanted to help me…" He stabbed his finger toward the mounds of paperwork stacked next to the computer screen.

She wrinkled her nose but couldn't argue—her new doctor had cleared her for light work at thirty-plus weeks, but warned her not to overdo it.

And when Annie asked her to help plan a large event at the café, that meant less time on her feet at the bakery—and more for her second job.

Hank rubbed his hand over his hair as he inhaled. When he exhaled through pursed lips, he seemed to search for the right words.

"Once everything is caught up—" he waved an arm at the mess on the workspace, "—you can join me in the shop."

Hank dismissed her to refill his mug. It took restraint not to behave like her six-year-old when *he* didn't get his way.

She reached for the thermos, filled from a pitcher she'd grabbed from the refrigerator that morning. One sip of the chilled water, and the telltale sweetness curled around her tongue.

Only Lacey Sweetwater Pershing could be behind the infamous matchmaking.

She hesitated, thermos poised.

On her and the mechanic?

She shook her head. The notion was beyond ridiculous.

But had it been a coincidence when they'd been seated side by side during Friday's dinner?

Plus, after they'd dropped the kids off in their respective Sunday school classrooms the previous morning, only two spots in the sanctuary "just happened" to be vacant—next to each other.

Coincidences, maybe. But with Sweetwater's most notorious meddler involved? Olive didn't think so.

She peered around the computer screen. Even with his supposedly packed schedule, Hank sure took his sweet time at the coffee station. First, he poured from the carafe, his back muscles shifting beneath his coveralls. Then he pursed his lips and blew across the surface of the brew. He took a sip and swished the coffee around in his mouth before swallowing.

She smirked. If motherhood had taught her anything, it was how to spot a dawdler. He was keeping tabs on her.

Lowering her eyes back to the figures, she adjusted herself on the swivel chair.

It felt like the two of them had settled into a smoother rhythm. She liked to think Pastor Mark's message at church had hit home—his sermon from Galatians on "Bear ye one another's burdens."

That thought alone motivated her to keep plugging through the mountain of paperwork. Once that was done, he couldn't keep her out of the shop.

Hank cleared his throat. "Okay, then—I'll leave you to it."

He disappeared into the shop, the faint scent of motor oil lingering behind.

The rest of her agreed-upon time passed at a snail's pace, broken up by a few customer drop-ins throughout the morning.

While she worked through the accounts payable and receivable— the pile finally beginning to shrink—her mind wandered.

After church, Lacey had invited her family to join her and the Pershings' toddler daughter, Ada Mae, at the preserve and sanctuary. That afternoon had been balmy, with highs in the forties— perfect for the kids to burn off some energy. Emerson had given them a private tour of the grounds, revealing a few persistent snow patches not yet touched by the sun.

Simon and Holly had weaved through the crowd to reach the

habitat housing the rescued tigers, Tony and Tina. Two staff members fed the large cats, accompanied by oohs and aahs from the onlookers.

Ada Mae had clung to her mother's hip while the two women stood off to the side. Lacey had casually remarked on Hank's tendency to drop everything to lend a hand to someone in need.

During the tour, Emerson also mentioned Hank's work on the live-in quarters at the preserve once she and Jack, Josie, and Dewey—their golden retriever—made their family official while waiting for their new home to be built.

On top of that, Hank had overseen renovations at Annie's café after Josh's freak accident the previous fall.

Like Mary in the Bible, Olive had gathered these small morsels about her temporary landlord and stored them in her heart.

Maybe he didn't see her as a project to fix, but that didn't mean *he* didn't deserve a little help, too.

A stab of guilt wedged itself below her rib cage. This time, she feared she'd taken advantage of the Pershings' kindness—especially when it related to helping out with her children.

Mrs. Spagnoletti chose that moment to sweep into the shop. She wore powder-blue eye shadow and bright pink lipstick, a smudge of which had settled on her front tooth.

Olive slipped off the stool and rounded the counter. "Mrs. S., hi!" She recalled the recently closed work orders Hank had reviewed with her. "Your car still running like a watch?"

Tugging on the front of her coveralls, she smiled at the woman.

Mrs. Spagnoletti fluttered a hand in front of her face and chuckled. "I'm sorry, child, but you are quite the vision."

A giggle escaped as Olive offered a half curtsy. "I know, right?"

The former town councilman's wife had been among the women who'd stopped by the ranch that first Sunday. The Spagnolettis had gained notoriety as the benefactors of several worthy causes—including the church's spring carnival.

Annie had pulled Olive aside early on to warn her: Mrs. S. had a knack for roping in unsuspecting volunteers like a cattle rustler.

"Is there something we can help you with, Mrs. S.?"

The woman tutted, her silver bob bouncing. "I'm depending on the councilman and Hank to handle the heavy lifting for the upcoming carnival."

Olive gave an absent nod.

For the past couple of days, she'd been toying with ideas to generate additional man—or woman—power at the garage, and she wanted to run them by Hank.

True, it would add to her workload, but it was one more way to repay his kindness.

"Hank's tied up at the moment, but—"

A cell phone chirped inside the roomy satchel dangling from Mrs. Spagnoletti's shoulder. She held up a manicured nail, then dove her other hand into the cloth bag.

"Have Big Country give me a call," she said, halfway across the lobby and out the door.

Hank barreled into the waiting area.

"Looks like I just dodged a bullet." He ran a hand over his beard and snickered.

Olive chuckled. "Not unless you're chomping at the bit to help at the spring carnival."

"You could say I earned quite a reputation at last year's Harvest Festival." He rolled his eyes, then finished the last of his coffee and unplugged the machine.

She returned to the stool and eased onto it. "Say, Hank—when Kate and I were talking after church yesterday, she mentioned the community college is offering an associate's degree in automotive service."

Hank raised his mug halfway to his mouth and met her eyes. "It's new this year. Why?"

Her pulse quickened. This could work.

But would Hank go for it?

"What if the garage extended an internship to students in the program?" Before falling asleep last night, she'd done some online research to support her case.

She tried to read Hank's expression—and failed.

The door swung open, and Constable Jack stepped in, his customary Stetson low on his brow and a wide smile stretching across his face.

"And with the Pershings' work with troubled youth at The Lodge, we could even start an apprenticeship program and—"

Hank's hand—large and steady—settled on her shoulder, making her heart flutter. Her mouth went dry. Probably dehydration.

He grunted. "Too much too soon, Olive."

Dismissing her, he turned to the constable. "Howdy, Jack."

"Hey, Big Country. Don't shoot down Olive's apprenticeship idea—especially since you've mentored at The Lodge."

Color rose on Hank's cheeks.

She'd picked up on that detail during the dinner party at the B and B. She shot Hank a smug told-you-so smile.

"Thank you, Constable."

She pinned her gaze on her boss. "I also have an idea to help minimize garage traffic."

Hank guffawed like the councilman himself. "You want to turn away business?" He tugged at his beard, his sky-blue eyes curious.

"Not in the literal sense." She reached for her thermos. "But if we offered classes on wintertime preventive maintenance, we might cut down on unnecessary tows and repairs."

Hank's hand dropped to his side like a ton of bricks, lips quirking into a skeptical line.

Jack nudged his Stetson off his forehead and belted out a laugh. "Number of guesses on how many women versus men sign up for a class taught by our local lumberjack?"

"And who's this *we*—" Hank added air quotes "—that's running these programs while work piles up?"

He gave a sharp shake of his head, snuffing out enthusiasm like a candle's flame.

Amid her excitement, she'd ignored logistics.

Still, the smile Hank offered softened the gruffness around his edges.

"I appreciate your ideas, Olive. I do. But I almost forgot—I've got a tow run."

He nodded at Jack. "Can she help you?"

The other man pointed at a shelf lined with batteries. "You bet."

Hank turned back to Olive, his expression tinged with concern. "You good to manage things on your own?"

Roman pushed himself off the floor, ears twitching.

She chuckled and dropped her hand to the Lab's silky head. "Yes—but are *you* game to take this big guy with you?"

His eyes sparkled. "You sure?"

She still couldn't believe Roman's uncanny affection for the mechanic. "He needs the fresh air and exercise."

Despite Hank's underwhelming reaction to her ideas, her pulse skipped a beat.

With him gone, she had free rein of the shop floor.

Finally.

She winked. "Don't worry about a thing—*boss*."

Jack clapped Hank on the shoulder. "See you later, Big Country."

"Say hi to Em." Hank disappeared out the front door into the crisp afternoon.

After ringing up the constable's purchase and reviewing the open work orders, she peeked over her shoulder before slipping onto the shop floor.

The familiar mix of burnt exhaust, dampness, and a metallic tang washed over her, and she sighed. "Granddad—can you believe it? I'm back in a garage," she whispered into the quiet.

Memories surfaced, pressing tears to her eyes—her and

Granddad tinkering in the old shed, evenings curled up on his ratty sofa with a supple leather Bible spread between them.

Thank You, Lord, for those precious moments.

Now wasn't the time to reminisce. No telling how long Hank would be gone.

She grabbed a wooden dolly and, after a few tries, found a semi-comfortable position on the hard board. Then she maneuvered under a run-of-the-mill four-door sedan and got to work. As she found her rhythm, everything else faded.

She didn't even hear the door squeak open—or the heavy clomp of boots on the cement floor.

"Mighty mackerel, woman—what do you think you're doing!"

Startled, Olive jerked. Her hand slipped, and black, viscous oil spilled onto the cement.

"Oh, no." She chomped her bottom lip as thick liquid pooled beside her.

The sharp intake of Hank's breath preceded the sight of his boots inches from her face.

"Olive! Are you hurt—wait, *don't move*! I'm calling 911!"

He dropped to his knees, ducking his head to peer beneath the car.

Then, sudden understanding lit her chest.

A burble of laughter rose and burst out.

"It's—not—*my*—water…" she wheezed between giggles.

The words tumbled out between peals of laughter and fresh tears that streamed into her hairline. She scootched the dolly from beneath the car and pushed into a seated position, brushing an errant tear clinging to her lashes.

But Hank wasn't laughing.

Alarm and confusion darkened his gaze.

"I thought—I was afraid that—"

He looked away, grief etched deep into the set of his jaw.

"I lost my sister a long time ago—"

He stood, slower than usual. With his back turned, she nearly missed his parting words.

"Stay out of the garage."

* * *

Though Hank never mentioned the incident again—not that day or the next—their dynamic shifted. Tension lingered like leftover smoke from a barbecue.

Guilt gnawed at her through the week. But it served a purpose—especially after she learned Monday's tow was caused by a driver who'd been completely unprepared.

With nine weeks until her due date, she had time to arrange both the internship and apprenticeship. Maybe even figure out how to tag-team the classes.

She just had to convince Hank.

That Friday morning, she smoothed her hand over the thin pages of Granddad's Bible resting on her lap and lifted her gaze heavenward. Roman, curled beside her, shifted his paw off her belly and gave a low whoof.

She didn't know the full story about Hank's sister, but it didn't stop the prayer from flowing.

"Please comfort Hank, Lord."

Her thoughts drifted. By the time she delivered, the car would be running, and hopefully her family would be well settled in their new home.

So why didn't that thought stir the same excitement it once had?

Chapter Five

Hank rolled the kinks from his neck.

He'd just closed the day's work orders after squirreling ten hours away in the garage. It wasn't until he'd removed the parts from Mrs. Greer's vehicle that his eyes glazed over, and he called it quits on conducting phone interviews for the open mechanic position.

Unimpressed with the candidates from Kate's job postings, he chucked the applications in the trash.

When he scrubbed his hand over the top of his head, the extra length still caught him off guard. It had always been easier to keep his hair cropped close since he'd grown it out, but he blamed a busy schedule for botching his routine.

Deep down, though, he blamed the sudden importance of his appearance on a certain woman who'd plowed into his life and roused his dormant heart.

He shook his head and powered down his computer with more gusto than necessary.

After he checked that the coffee maker was turned off, his cell phone chirped. He peeked at the screen and exhaled a sigh of relief.

"Hey, coz."

"Big Country! What did I hear about teaching classes now?" Gordie chuckled.

His cousin had no doubt spotted Olive's handiwork on social media and the Facebook page she'd created for the garage.

"Our temporary part-timer thinks preventive maintenance will give us more time to work on higher-priority jobs."

That was her reasoning behind his agreeing to run with her ideas.

His recent tow had solidified that decision—since it could've been avoided with basic preventive training.

"Us, huh? Sounds like Manny's already been replaced."

Hank snorted. "Did I mention she's also my very pregnant houseguest—with two kids and a dog?"

The idea of hiring Olive full-time would be humorous—if he hadn't seen the mediocre job applications with his own two eyes.

"What happened to equal opportunity, Hank?" Gordie's tone edged toward earnest.

"Either way, I can't wait to meet Miss Hart. And what about selling the ranch?"

"What about it?"

Truth was, his plans to sell the ranch for funds to expand the garage had taken a back seat.

His house felt more like a home these days.

At the realization, his heart flipped.

"No reason. Just curious. So, have you let her work in the bays yet?"

Gordie's question hit the target.

Now that she'd finished the administrative tasks, he'd used up his excuses.

Granted, he only had her word about her automobile expertise— but she'd nailed the issue with her car, which he confirmed with a quick check.

Plus, despite her doctor's support, he worried about her welfare and pushed back every time she gazed longingly at the shop door.

Not to mention the scare she'd given him when he thought her water had broken underneath the vehicle—dredging up memories of not saving his sister in time. If only he'd known Rosie had been sneaking out with his truck, its bald tires no match for a blizzard—maybe he could've stopped her before the accident stole her life.

Gordie cleared his throat, drawing Hank from the dark turn his thoughts had taken.

"Maybe early next week…if she's feeling up to it," Hank said. He snickered, adding, "Let's see what she's made of during the class we're tag-teaming."

Gordie let out a low whistle. "She must be a pretty special gal for you to agree to these changes."

Hank rolled his eyes. "You're way off base, coz." Yet he'd be lying if he denied the truth—she'd gotten under his skin. "The woman carries more baggage than I do."

"I find that hard to believe—but if that's how you live with yourself." He chortled. "Look, I've got to run, but I trust your decisions."

The call ended right after Gordie shared his plan to shift into the role of silent partner once staffing was under control.

No surprise. Gordie's aging mother and her Montana farm came first.

Hank crossed the lobby to lock up. But his cousin's hands-off approach didn't help with the staffing shortage.

At the door, his hand hovered over the knob; strength seeped out of him. But then Olive's image came to mind, lifting his spirits.

Which should've troubled him even more than Gordie's announcement—because the last thing he needed was another distraction.

Behind the wheel of his tow truck, he fought the Friday evening traffic toward the two-lane highway and his ranch.

Should he have given Olive a heads-up that he was heading back early?

His emotions waged war with his conscience.

Slowing for a deer that crossed the road with two speckled fawns at her side, he tugged on his beard.

A quick call to the ranch to let her know he'd knocked off ahead of schedule would take all of a minute.

Since when did he need to account for his whereabouts? It was his place, wasn't it?

But he knew it was more than that. The ranch had taken on a life of its own.

That acknowledgment chiseled away at the bricks surrounding his heart.

Inch by inch, the Harts' presence lessened his grief—and gave him another excuse to say yes to Olive's ideas for the garage.

At least that's what he told himself, the pines a blur as he zipped past them.

Just as he rolled onto his driveway, the crunch of gravel under his tires, his cell phone dinged with a text.

Once parked in the garage, he read the group message from Mrs. Spagnoletti confirming his and Persh's help with the spring carnival.

The dunk tank his friend had built for last year's Fourth of July Bash popped into his head. Before that, his work for the Harvest Festival.

He chuckled. That woman had a way with persuasion.

Slamming the door behind him, he lumbered into the breezeway. It wasn't until he kicked off his boots that his intuition pricked.

No jangle of dog tags.

No savory scents wafting from the kitchen.

Silence greeted him.

He shed his coveralls, a sense of alarm ratcheting his pulse.

After dropping his soiled outerwear atop the washing machine, he entered the dining area—

And stopped dead in his tracks.

Was *gobsmacked* the right word?

A glance at the windows to check for broken glass.

Negative.

But he'd pledge on Olive's Granddad's Bible that a microburst had touched down square in the middle of his home.

Toys, clothing, blankets, and sheets—doubling as a fort—covered every surface.

Remnants from the day's meals dried on dishes littering the counter.

Until now, despite his protests, Olive had kept the place spotless.

Which meant one thing.

Something happened.

Laughter and high-pitched squeals from outside pierced his awareness.

Or not.

He swung his gaze from the interior carnage to the picture window at the far end of the living room.

There, beyond the white picket fence, stood an abandoned claw-foot bathtub—an ancient salt lick dangling from its side—once a watering trough for the family's cows and horses.

He spotted Olive propped on a hay bale in front of a stall, and relief punctured the cloud of dread.

She watched Holly and Simon take turns kicking a rubber ball across the crusted mud. With tongue lolling, Roman weaved between their legs.

Hank's blood pounded in his ears, transporting him back to the Valentine's Day blizzard, the four of them huddled for safety.

The last brick fell then, crumbling into rubble to expose a heart marked by grief and loss.

And then she raised her eyes, as if she felt the weight of his stare.

The radiant smile she'd leveled at her kids slipped. Her lips formed the letter O, her expressive eyes rounding.

Maybe with surprise—or something else.

Realization slammed into him.

I should've called first.

He didn't give a lick of care about the condition of his home—

But Olive's flushed face said she felt otherwise.

The Lab's big head lifted, and he yipped.

Yup, boy.

Time to move his stuff into the doghouse until his house-guests moved out.

Olive corralled Simon and Holly surprisingly fast, considering.

Once in the breezeway, she whispered to the kids, and they scurried down the hall without a peep.

She slipped off her coat and boots, then faced him.

"I'm sorry about the mess, Hank—if I'd known you were coming home early—"

Ducking her head, she shuffled past him. "Dinner will be ready in thirty or less—plenty of time to get washed up."

She busied herself clearing the counter, her back to him.

His gut twisted.

Entering the kitchen, he covered her hand with his as she tugged on the fridge handle. Her pulse jumped at his touch.

"Olive—I should've called first."

Had her skin always been this soft?

He coughed under his breath. "It's really no big deal."

With superhuman effort, he pulled his hand away.

Slowly, she peered up at him with an expression he couldn't read.

He searched her golden eyes—and a zing of awareness struck him in the solar plexus.

Clearing his throat, he took a step back. What was he thinking? The last thing he needed was to open a can of worms with the single mother.

"How can I help—never mind," he muttered, putting distance between them. "I know just the thing."

He followed the jangle of Roman's tags down the hallway and found Holly and Simon in their room, already dressed in their pajamas.

In record time, the three of them tidied up the living area, earning him a surprise peck on the cheek from Olive. Even the delicious chili she served paled to the warmth of her velvety touch sinking into the coarse scruff of his beard.

The four of them ate in relative silence for several minutes, but once Roman scooted beneath the table to forage for scraps, the kids' afternoon adventures spilled out of them.

At the far end of the stalls, they'd discovered the abandoned barn where he'd stored the Harts' belongings the night of the blizzard, a night that still lingered in his mind.

How did he feel about opening the door wider to the past that held so much grief?

"Have you considered rehabbing that old barn?"

Olive's question redirected his thoughts. When she pressed a napkin to her lips, his fingers itched to touch the spot on his cheek where she kissed him.

A chunk of ground turkey lodged in his throat, and he pounded his fist against his chest.

Buying time.

"Not a priority since my folks passed."

"We pretended it's a castle and Mommy's the princess," Holly added, her smile extra wide to show off the new gap where a front tooth used to be.

Olive let out a nervous chuckle. "The space has so much potential, though." Her gaze turned dreamy.

Truth was, once upon a time, his mother had imagined the barn as a place to host guests and special events. That dream had died with her and his dad.

"It's been a while," he grunted.

The chair scraped the floorboards as he stood to gather the dishes, cutting off Olive's usual protests.

She cast him a look that held gratitude and a hint of curiosity as she chewed a thick slab of whole wheat bread from the bakery.

Didn't matter what she thought about the barn anyway. Not when it conveyed with the property—if he went through with the sale.

While he boxed up the leftovers, she corralled the kids for bedtime stories and prayers.

Soon, her soft footfalls signaled her return.

She wore a faded green robe that had seen better days, but it brought out the flecks of cinnamon in her eyes as she joined him at the sink full of hot, soapy water.

To an outsider, it might look domestic.

He scolded himself.

This arrangement—whatever you wanted to call it—was temporary.

Olive's car would be back in commission soon. The furnace in the studio apartment replaced.

Then he'd move back into his space at the garage.

"Between living with my mother and my ex-husband—"

Her voice was soft, and something in it told him what she was about to say would cost her. He strained not to miss a word.

"I was always treated like a burden…"

His chest tightened, and he turned to face her. She clenched a Hooked on Fishing dish towel between her fingers.

"Donny—the children's father—left us for someone else, my granddad died, and—"

She hiccupped, clutching the towel to her chest. "We lost everything," she whispered.

Her admission sparked a flare of anger—tempered by how her teeth caught her bottom lip.

Lord, what kind of man would do that to a woman?

Her constant efforts not to inconvenience anyone suddenly made sense.

His hands stilled, and the pot he was scrubbing dipped below the surface of the suds.

He searched her eyes, now misted with unshed tears.

"Okay if I say something?"

She gave a small nod.

"From where I stand, your ex left you with all the burdens."

She gasped, as if his words struck a nerve.

"Granddad and the kids have *never* been a burden," she snapped, her tone sharp.

"Olive—that's not what I meant."

He placed a sudsy hand over hers.

She schooled her features and slipped her hand from his, then turned and fled the room—leaving behind her floral scent and the hurt in her eyes.

Roman's knowing gaze followed her, his dark eyes full of accusation from beneath a kitchen chair.

"I know, boy."

He'd done it again.

In that moment, he was forced to admit that it wasn't the Harts' problems keeping him up at night.

His feelings for Olive and her family weren't just real.

They were dangerous.

Because he'd unwittingly put his own heart in jeopardy.

Four days later, Olive was still berating herself for unloading her family's baggage on Hank.

She'd been flummoxed since he'd turned up unannounced at the ranch that Friday evening.

Good grief, it's not like she expected the man to give her a play-by-play of his schedule—he lived there.

She tucked a few loose strands of hair into an unruly top-knot and appraised her reflection in the shop's bathroom mirror.

The corners of her mouth dipped. But the once-dormant butterflies behind her rib cage refused to cooperate.

Her mind spun in circles, replaying that evening—standing side by side at the kitchen sink.

His gentle attempt to correct her misunderstanding.

But the seed had been planted when he'd suggested her kids—her granddad—had been a burden.

And after a lifetime of listening to Donny complain about being saddled down with her "and the lot of them," she'd jumped to conclusions.

Not that Hank's actions hadn't spoken louder than words from day one. He was patient to a fault, for one thing—nothing like her ex.

Hank's compassion had triggered her reaction—the need to untangle herself from his intense gaze.

"Forgive me for finding fault, Lord." Remorse settled heavily in her spirit. "When all I should feel is gratitude for Hank's generosity."

He'd even been extra sweet since then, backpedaling in quiet, practical ways. She'd waved off her own hurt, blamed her hormones—but the crisp pink uniform he'd left on the kitchen table over the weekend had felt like a peace offering, and the gesture had melted her anyway.

She drew in a deep breath and released it slowly, smoothing her hands across the front of her coveralls—the baby bump rounding more each day. A small smile reached her eyes at the sight of it.

"Ready for showtime, partner?" Hank's voice came from the other side of the closed door.

Her heart kicked up, and the butterflies took flight. She'd like to blame them on the inaugural class they were facilitating that morning. But she suspected they had more to do with the timbre of Hank's voice—the way it vibrated beneath the soles of her boots.

"Ready or not!"

They expected at least a dozen participants from the Facebook event she'd posted, plus the announcement at church.

Not only did she hope to relieve the garage from unnecessary service calls, but she wanted to shine in front of her boss and prove her granddad had taught her well.

She rubbed her belly with one hand.

Okay, baby, let's show them what we're made of.

With the other, she grasped the door handle and pulled—praying for the Lord's favor on the morning ahead.

She entered the empty hallway and stepped through the door into the nearest garage bay.

At the front, a parked vehicle held center stage. In the rear, the overhead door hung open on its tracks.

A portable table lined one wall where Annie had set out pastries and carafes filled with specialty coffees, hot water for tea, and creamy cocoa to combat the midmorning chill.

To her surprise, the two rows of folding chairs were each occupied by class participants—many she recognized from her short time in town.

Huh.

She'd expected a good turnout. But this?

As she sank her palms into her low back to ease a new ache, she pressed her lips together to keep from giggling out loud.

The constable had called it.

One lone male made up the twelve attendees—a potential apprentice the Pershings had recommended for the program she'd proposed.

She spotted Hank at the front of the room.

He tugged on his beard with one hand, his neck mottling.

If his discomfort wasn't so painful to observe, she'd totally rate the rubbernecking a nine out of ten in hilarity.

She crossed the floor, her lips forming a smirk. "Sorry, I'm a little late."

The panic-stricken expression in Hank's eyes was replaced by relief.

Seriously, what had the man expected?

Especially since his copper-colored hair had grown out a bit and he'd trimmed his beard.

Even dressed in coveralls, the mechanic was a walking advertisement for rugged appeal.

What am I doing?

She tamped down thoughts she had no business entertaining. Clearing her throat, she made eye contact with each attendee.

"Welcome to Preventive Auto Maintenance 101."

The next forty-five minutes flew by as she and Hank demonstrated basic vehicle upkeep—everything from checking fluid levels and tire pressure to removing and changing a flat tire for a spare.

During a fifteen-minute Q and A session at the end of the class, Ms. Reed—the town's librarian—raised her hand.

Olive pointed at the woman, whose bright red lipstick would've fit in better on a night out.

Ms. Reed turned her full attention to Hank.

"Big Country, when I leave for work every day, there's fluid on my driveway."

She didn't really just flutter her thick lashes…

"My brother told me it's the oil or the power steering fluid."

It was so quiet you could hear a pin drop.

Hank cleared his throat. "Good question—I'll let my partner address that one."

He faced Olive with an unmistakable gleam in his eye.

He's challenging me.

She squared her shoulders.

Oh—it's on, mister.

Just then, she flashed back to the recent oil spill when he'd startled her—after she'd snuck into the garage.

But in the end, he'd commended her for a job well done—after she'd promised not to pull something like that again.

Now, though, she sensed that if she passed this test of sorts, it'd be harder for Hank to refuse her help on the shop floor.

She smiled widely, tucking away her nerves under his watchful eye and turning toward the class.

"I'm glad you asked." She met the librarian's shuttered gaze, a pout on her red lips.

"While both are common leaks—it's important to note that power steering fluid is similar in color to engine oil."

She paused, drawing from her granddad's lessons.

"The key is to look for exactly where the leak originated—as well as check your power steering fluid levels and engine oil to verify if either is running low."

Though all eyes were fixed on her, there was only one person in the room she hoped to impress.

"Finally—if the fluid is bright in color, the culprit is most likely your coolant."

She peeked over her shoulder and caught Hank's eye. He nodded, a sparkle in his blue gaze that read as approval in her owner's manual.

The fluttering in her belly started up again as the class clapped and began moving toward the refreshment table.

All except for Ms. Reed, who cornered Hank while he gathered folding chairs.

Olive overheard him invite her to schedule an appointment in the lobby on her way out. She took that as her cue to duck into the ladies' room.

Once everyone had filed out, she poked her head into the garage. Hank had returned the shop to working order and looked up.

"What'd you think, boss?"

He grunted, with less than his usual bravado—a spark of pride in his grin.

"Not bad."

Her heart soared.

As she eased the door closed, Hank shouted.

"Hey—Olive?"

She arched an eyebrow. In two strides, he joined her at the shop entrance—a veritable battle of some kind going on behind his eyes.

Had she messed up somehow? Read more into his assessment than she should have?

She held her breath, eyes locked on how his beard highlighted the depths of blue.

He nodded once, then twice—as if he'd come to a decision.

"You wouldn't want to change out the cabin filter on Emerson's SUV…?" His jaw relaxed, and he winked.

Her pulse picked up just as her baby shifted.

We did it!

If only Granddad could see her now.

A soft ache pierced her heart over her loss.

At the same time, she sensed her win had come at a cost behind Hank's not-so-casual offer.

Because of that, she took his lead and slipped into a companionable silence as they worked on their respective jobs until it was time to pick up Holly and Simon from school.

Strapped in the back seat of the tow truck, the kids chattered nonstop about an upcoming fishing contest announced during church on Sunday and again at school assembly that morning. But Olive was still camped out on cloud nine and barely heard a word.

Before she knew it, they were rolling onto the pavement in front of the B and B.

"Thanks, Mr. Big!" Simon and Holly tumbled from the vehicle and raced each other up the walkway.

Hank watched the kids for a couple of beats, his brows tented.

Olive sensed the wheels turning inside that head of his.

Then he climbed out and rounded the front bumper—a routine he'd established early on.

Pulling the passenger door open, he reached in to help her down.

But when his calloused palm grazed her forearm, a shiver rippled through her—despite the pre-spring sunshine warming her exposed neck.

Before they'd left the shop, she'd changed out of her grease-stained coveralls into an oversized, lightweight sweatshirt. An arrow and the phrase Baby on Board were appliqued across the front—though her belly made the message obvious.

As soon as her soles touched the ground, he released her.

The look in his clear blue eyes sent her butterflies fluttering again.

Surely it was just the hormones making her emotions around her boss so topsy-turvy.

He dipped his head, then opened and closed his mouth.

Had something shifted since he'd inspected her work in the garage?

She ran through a few possibilities but came up empty-handed.

Rocking back on his heels, he cleared his throat. "Think the kids would wanna enter the fishing contest next weekend at the lake?"

Her foot slipped from cloud nine.

"Oh, Hank." Her lips dipped into a frown. "To my granddad's utter disappointment, that was the one skill I never mastered."

His eyes twinkled—reminding her of Simon at bedtime, recounting his day's adventures.

Stretching one arm wide, he bowed. "Look no further—fishing just happens to be another of my superpowers."

He puffed out his broad chest, then reached into the front seat to grab her purse. As he looped the strap over her shoulder, her chest swelled at the casual gesture.

The man had already done so much.

"Give it some thought—and don't worry about the entry fee."

"But—"

"Trust me." He chuckled. "The prize money will more than cover it."

He bumped her door shut—a tremble rolling through her as his forearm brushed her side.

With a lift of his hand in a silly salute, he turned and climbed back into the tow truck. By the time she reached the inn's front entrance, he was already backing out of the lot.

"Well, come in, come in!"

Lacey stood in the doorway, her wide smile lighting up her face.

The woman's emerald eyes sparkled with what Olive recognized as matchmaking mischief.

She stifled a snort as Lacey pulled her into a loose embrace and ushered her inside.

The look her new friend gave her could only mean one thing.

And the last thing Olive needed was a new man in her life.

"Welcome to the planning committee, Olive." Miss Marie smiled from her spot at the dining table.

"It's good to see you again," said Kate, the constable's half-sister, patting the empty chair beside her.

"Hi there, momma." Annie pushed her black frames higher on her nose.

Olive set her purse on the table and sank into the seat. "Thanks for including me," she said, craning her neck to take it all in.

Lacey bustled up to the table, her long skirt swishing around her ankles. "Simon and Holly are outside with Josie and her big brother, Anthony." Her green eyes twinkled. "So let's get this party started while the babies sleep."

"So Olive—" Annie folded her hands on the table "—we were thinking, since your hands are already full…"

A sigh of relief bubbled in her chest. When she'd agreed to sit in on the spring carnival committee, she questioned her sanity. But she'd wanted to help—it was the least she could do to thank the townsfolk for their warm welcome.

Not that she'd ever intended to get attached. Not when her gig at the bakery was only temporary.

Miss Marie nodded, her silver hair catching the afternoon light. "If you can swing it, we'd need you to make a last-minute grocery run before the event."

That could work.

If she had her wheels.

And it would satisfy her doctor, who'd recently advised her to cut back her work hours.

"That would be perfect." Olive bit into a thick slice of moist banana bread from the bakery, the morsel melting on her tongue. "I can't believe this is gluten- and dairy-free!"

Doc Wells—Emerson—pushed through the swinging doors, her mahogany braid slung over her shoulder.

"Right?" She pointed at the loaf. "When I told Annie about Anthony's gluten intolerance, she started experimenting with different recipes for folks with food allergies."

The baker's cheeks flushed a pretty pink. "Not only that…" Annie patted her baby bump, much smaller than Olive's. "Since I'll be a momma of two soon, I'm motivated to include healthier options on the menu."

Lacey grabbed a pitcher from the table, her eyes gleaming with mischief.

"More sweet water, anyone?"

The four women giggled, their eyes focusing squarely on Olive. Her skin heated under their playful gazes.

"What?"

Kate chuckled. "Don't tell me you haven't heard about the infamous town legend?"

Oh, that.

"Of course. But since I'm not in the market to replace my ex—"

So why did a sudden image of Hank make her throat grow dry?

Grabbing the closest glass—etched with a forest scene—she gulped down the chilled liquid.

Beside her, Miss Marie reached out to pat her hand.

"Pay no never mind to our teasing, dear." Fine wrinkles fanned out from her kind eyes. "But if you ever change your mind—we can vouch for Big Country's big heart."

Miss Marie wasn't wrong. Olive had witnessed it time and again.

That wasn't the issue.

Hank had made it clear. Hadn't he?

Or maybe she'd imagined it—that he was counting the days until he was no longer responsible for her family's well-being.

Not that it explained her reaction to Ms. Reed's flirtation during class.

Nor did it help that the town grapevine confirmed the single woman also set her sights on the fire chief last year.

Before Josh discovered his perfect match in the town's baker.

Brushing away an imaginary crumb, Olive pasted on a smile.

"I'm pretty sure Hank will be relieved when my brood is out of his hair."

Which should be soon.

Just that week, Annie had shared the good news—the furnace was expected to be installed within the week. Olive had offered to move in sooner since the days were warming up, but the night-time lows still made heat necessary. Still, she couldn't shake the memory of the faint scratching she'd heard near the furnace last time she'd been in the back room. Whatever it had been, it had added an edge of unease to her anticipation.

Moving from the ranch's sprawling space to a tiny studio would be an adjustment, but her family needed it.

"Speaking of hair—I don't think I've ever seen him with it this long." Annie helped herself to a second slice of bread.

Lacey batted a fiery curl from her cheek and giggled. "I guess there's a first time for everything."

The conspiratorial looks passing between the women didn't escape Olive's notice, just as raised voices and the thunder of little feet interrupted the moment.

The distraction couldn't have come at a better time as all eyes turned toward the kitchen.

"Mr. Big is our new daddy!"

Olive gasped at Holly's familiar voice, her palm flying to her mouth as every woman at the table stared—eyebrows nearly vanishing into their hairlines.

"I got a new mommy, too!" Josie added, her voice brimming with pride as the kids traipsed through the swinging doors in stocking feet.

"Mommy!"

Holly skipped over and rested her cheek against Olive's abdomen, then ran off to join her friends in the living room—her innocent comment already forgotten.

But not by Olive.

It had become all too clear—like the sparkling sweet water served by the town matchmaker—that the tumultuous emotions she felt around Hank were inconsequential.

Not when she'd unwittingly let her children believe their arrangement was something more than temporary—a false impression she had to correct.

Before it bloomed into childlike hopes that would inevitably crash.

Even then, Olive feared it was already too late.

Because she, too, had started to believe in happy endings.

Chapter Six

"Mr. Big, Mr. Big—is this how you do it?"

Holly Hart's gap-toothed grin tugged on the grizzled edges of Hank's heart as he appraised the thick, juicy worm wriggling at the end of the hook she clutched between her fingers.

"Here's the right way!" Simon brandished his baited line—the hook swinging perilously close to his sister's face.

Hank swallowed a gasp.

Their mother would *so* not appreciate an ER visit on his watch.

Grasping a pole in each hand, he crouched on the bank of Sweetwater Lake where they'd staked their claim.

He inhaled slowly, keeping his tone gentle.

"Kids—what's the number one rule?"

He looked them both in the eyes.

"Always wear a life jacket!" Simon grinned, eager for praise.

"Don't get hooked!" Holly chimed in.

He didn't bother suppressing a chuckle.

"You're both right—now watch how I cast my line into the water."

He demonstrated the proper technique—skills his father had taught him before he could even walk—all while keeping one eye on Olive.

At the moment, she stood a few yards away on the sandy shoreline, chatting with Lacey. According to Persh, the on-site film crew had just wrapped up their photo shoot at the B and B, giving the couple a well-earned reprieve from innkeeper duties.

The kids' mom blended in with the contest participants who'd arrived at dawn, bundled in jackets and gloves.

But now that the late-morning sun had warmed the air, outerwear had been traded for sunscreen.

"Mr. Big?"

Holly tugged on his fishing vest, and he refocused on the lesson—casting a perfect arc with his line.

Still, he sneaked another look at Olive.

She wore baggy denim jeans, rolled up at the ankles, and canvas shoes on her feet. An oversized T-shirt did nothing to disguise her pregnancy.

An unguarded smile tilted her lips, and his heart hitched at how her skin glowed.

Until her gaze caught his.

Something had changed. And not in a good way.

The ease of their temporary arrangement—at home and in the garage—had settled into a comfortable rhythm.

Which was why her sudden avoidance these past few days felt…off.

At first, he'd chalked it up to his comment—suggesting her granddad and kids were burdens after her ex walked out. He hadn't meant it that way. He'd just meant she wasn't a burden—but a woman carrying far too much on her own.

Or maybe she'd noticed how fast his heart had been pounding when they'd stood mere inches apart at the sink.

He gulped, picturing the spray of freckles scattered across her nose.

Still, things had seemed okay after he'd surprised her with those brand-spanking-new pink coveralls.

That is—until he'd picked up her and the kids from the inn after their first class at the garage.

"When're we gonna catch a fishie, Mr. Big?"

Holly pointed at a nearby contestant reeling in a decent-sized speckled trout.

"What did I tell you about patience, guys?"

Hank tugged on the pom topping the knit cap Holly wore askew.

Simon plopped down on the sand, eyes glued to rib red-and-white bobber floating on the lake's glossy surface.

"Waiting develops character," the boy said solemnly.

Hank's chest swelled.

Despite how little Olive shared about the kids' father, her inner strength—and how she parented with equal parts grace and grit—never failed to impress him.

His admiration for her kept growing.

So did his fondness for Holly and Simon.

Roman whoofed, and Hank chuckled under his breath.

And the big lug, too.

His attention drifted back to Olive.

She stepped away from the Pershings with a little wave, closing the distance between them with one slender hand resting gently on her abdomen.

It slammed into him—the whiff of her floral scent when he'd strapped her purse across her shoulder in the inn's parking lot, golden eyes sparkling with appreciation.

That's when he'd given in to a last-minute detour and pulled around to The Lodge—a refurbished A-frame behind the B and B.

"Hey, you two—how are my little fisher people?"

Hank was pulled from his thoughts by Olive's arrival—her hair gathered in a loose ponytail, a few strands framing a makeup-free face, making her look every bit a college student.

Holly launched herself at Olive.

"Mommy, I touched a worm!"

Grinning from ear to ear, the little girl clutched Olive's hand and tugged her toward where the kids' poles were propped in the ground with fishing rod holders.

When Olive's eyes met his, a veil seemed to fall. Her lips curved into a soft smile.

He was powerless to stop the hitch behind his rib cage.

"Thank you," she mouthed, before turning her attention to Simon and Holly.

From nearby, he watched the three of them on the bank. At the same time, Persh's scrutiny—next to Lacey and their daughter—dragged his thoughts back to that afternoon's visit.

If the councilman wasn't busy with town business, he could usually be found at the after-school program for troubled youth he and Lacey ran at The Lodge or acting as the inn's handyman.

The same inn where it all began—when Lacey's grandparents had stepped into Persh's life and changed the trajectory of an impressionable preteen.

Early on in The Lodge's inception, Hank had served as a Big Brother to a teen who'd since aged out of the program and now attended Sweetwater Community College.

But Hank had never felt worthy of offering guidance to other young men—not after failing to protect his sister.

Not after every failed attempt at a lasting relationship.

He reeled in his thoughts before they veered into turbulent waters—his gaze refocusing on the kids and their mom.

Because of them, he'd been forced to confront his past, which was why he'd sought out Persh as a sounding board—though Hank had a few more birthdays tucked under his tool belt than both the constable and the councilman.

"Mr. Big—I got a bite!"

Simon sat cross-legged, then shot straight up like a jack-in-the-box, arms flapping.

"Okay, son, hold on."

Pressing pause on his mental meandering, Hank helped the boy reel in a tiny sunfish, its scales catching the light like a kaleidoscope.

"Okay if I get a quick picture?"

Olive's cheeks were tinted with a becoming pink as she pointed her phone camera at Simon—the buttons on the boy's shirt nearly popping off as he brandished his catch.

She snapped a series of photos, then Hank showed the boy how to release the fish into the water.

Since the contest was classified as catch and release, the goal was to tally the most catches during the designated hours.

Holly yawned—her lips opening as wide as the fish they'd just set free.

He'd wondered how much longer the kids would last.

"Who's hungry?"

Olive flicked her wrist toward the cooler she'd packed earlier.

Had it been just this morning?

It felt more like days than hours since they'd hauled it to the beach beneath the yellow, orange, and red rays that dazzled the early morning arrivals.

"Yay!"

Both kids abandoned their poles, eager to help Olive arrange yogurt and sliced fruit, fresh butter, and slabs of the bakery's leftover banana bread on a soft blanket spread on the ground.

The three of them dug in with gusto.

With one eye on the poles, Hank's thoughts drifted back to his conversation with Persh.

He'd interrupted the councilman mid-demonstration—Persh was showing a group of young men how to sand a wooden platform he'd built for the spring carnival's bean bag toss.

Satisfied his instructions had landed, Persh grabbed two glass bottles and thrust one into Hank's hand.

The labels advertised the inn's sweet water—pumped from a proprietary aquifer dating back hundreds of years.

Hank had accepted the offering with a roll of his eyes.

Once jilted by the legend, he put little stock into the theory that there was something special in the sweet water.

"You sure there isn't more happening between you and your houseguest?"

Persh had cocked a brow—let the silence build.

With one hand buried in the trimmed scruff of his beard,

Hank had denied it up and down—the adage, *thou dost protest too much*, ringing in his ears.

All he'd done was unload his concerns about Olive and her situation.

Except…his cousin had hinted at something similar right before, he mentioned his plans to step down as an active partner.

Hank had been forced to face the reality of the garage's future.

Even with Olive's part-time help, time wasn't on his side.

Not when the programs she'd spearheaded would take weeks—maybe months—to implement.

Which brought him full circle.

Once the Harts moved off the ranch, he had to move forward and sell it to secure the funds he needed.

Persh's words played back in his mind again.

"You wanna know what I think?"

The councilman had dropped a piece of sandpaper on a large folding table in The Lodge's multipurpose room—normally used for the inn's weekly jam sessions.

As usual, Persh hadn't waited for a reply.

Rubbing his palm across his goatee, he'd looked Hank in the eye.

"It's high time you stop trying to fix everyone else's problems. Leave 'em to the Master Mechanic."

He couldn't deny the truth in his friend's words.

Roman leaped at a bird hopping near the picnic blanket—tugging Hank's attention back to the Harts.

His heart squeezed at the sight, confirming everything Persh had said.

Motorboats powered across the glassy lake, and Hank's thoughts drifted to his parents' deaths—how he'd taken on the role of parent to Rosie and manager of the ranch.

Taken on whatever needed fixing.

No, he didn't believe God held him responsible for the accident that claimed his sister's life.

Still, he'd made it his mission to protect others.

At all costs.

It sure didn't help in the relationship department. But it made him a good mechanic.

As far as the Harts?

They meant more to him than any fix-it project.

He'd told himself he'd be glad when things returned to normal, when the house was quiet again.

So why doesn't that thought comfort me?

Olive waved at him, pointing to the blanket.

The smile crossing her face did funny things to his pulse, and he swallowed.

His boots sank into the sandy bank as he crossed to the blanket and dropped onto the edge.

"Here, try this." She held out a slab of banana bread.

He plucked it from her hand, careful not to touch.

Simon and Holly skipped rocks at the water's edge—their giggles confirming his worst fear: he was in deep, uncharted waters.

Olive's gaze swept over the trees lining the shoreline, teeming with contestants.

"It's hard to believe a month ago this—" she spread her arms wide "—was all covered in snow."

He grunted softly, his mind grasping for anything other than the breeze dancing through strands of caramel and honey framing her face.

She patted his knee, and his eyes dropped to the spot.

"So why is a good guy like you still single?"

Her question landed hook, line, and sinker—smacking him square in the solar plexus.

Had she not heard through the town grapevine?

It wasn't exactly a secret that his former fiancée left him at the altar.

But he needed her to hear the truth from *him*.

At least they were speaking again.

Thank You, Lord, for small graces.

Or maybe she *had* heard, and that's the reason she'd kept her distance this week.

Either way, he couldn't remember the workdays ever dragging so much.

Tugging off his ball cap, he scratched the top of his head and exhaled.

"Me and my high school sweetheart were gonna get married when Rosie—my kid sister—was killed."

He paused, throat tightening as the past rose to meet him.

Still, it didn't stop him from noticing how the golden flecks in Olive's eyes dimmed.

His whole body shuddered. The memories slammed into him.

"And she—my fiancée—"

What more was there to say?

"Hank—"

His name on her lips was almost his undoing.

"She broke off the wedding."

He shrugged—a simple gesture that didn't come close to hiding the sting.

"Let's just say I haven't been the most pleasant to be with since then."

He bit back a grunt. More like *hyper*-protective.

That's what Kelly had written in her Dear John letter all those years ago.

"That had to have been devastating."

Olive's gaze drifted to the shoreline. He studied her profile, the sadness tugging at her lips.

He knew her story. Her loss.

Still, Kelly's leaving had only validated what he believed about himself.

And he refused to risk his heart again—no matter what longings Olive and her family stirred in him.

Longing for more than a back room at the garage. More than an empty house.

When Olive faced him again, her eyes shot straight to his heart.

He tugged on his beard. He'd overshared. Big time.

Dragging his gaze away, he stabbed a finger toward the lake.

"The *real* devastating thing? We still need to haul in a bucket full of fish."

Compassion softened Olive's gaze as he rose, twisting something deep in his gut.

Brushing off the seat of his cargo pants, he looked to the water.

"Ready to win this contest, kids?"

Both children dropped their stones and raced to the blanket—Roman on their heels, tail wagging at warp speed.

He snuck a peek at their mother.

Was that pity flashing across her face?

He winced, lowering his gaze to the water bottles in her hands. Her sympathy wasn't welcome.

Nor was the town matchmaker's behind-the-scenes meddling—well-intentioned or not.

So why had he waited to share his story with Olive? He didn't know. Afraid he'd scare her off too soon? Or was it something else entirely? Her SUV was running again—he'd even detailed it yesterday, inside and out, right down to the undercarriage. And the apartment was nearly ready. She was free to go. No debt left to settle.

But now there was no reason to keep it to himself—especially when she had no reason to stay.

Olive's internal clock struggled to catch up. Peering out the bakery's floor-to-ceiling picture window, she stifled a yawn. In the background, the Town Square historic office building stood shrouded in fog. Over the past few days, a chill had settled in, carried in with the spring rains and lingering dampness.

As a favor to Annie, she'd opened the shop at dark thirty that morning—though she wouldn't have minded a few more minutes of shut-eye.

But since Hank's Sunday afternoon surprise—handing her the keys to her SUV—juggling work schedules around the kids' drop-off and pickups was a lot easier.

The return of her wheels couldn't have come at a better time.

"Mommy, can you look at my paper?"

From the high-top table where both kids were busy, Holly waved a colorful activity sheet. Backpack straps dangled from the chairs, crumbs from toasted egg and sausage sandwiches littered two plates, and Simon's half-finished juice sat forgotten beside him.

The kitchen timer dinged.

"Give me a few minutes, sweetie." Olive turned from the window and smiled at her daughter.

As she slipped through the café doors, hints of cinnamon and nutmeg welcomed her into the warm space. Tugging oven mitts over her slightly swollen fingers and savoring the scent, Olive's eyes flicked to the back room.

The last time she'd been back there, Simon had frozen mid-step. "Did you hear that, Mom?"

Holly had nodded, eyes wide. "Something's running around in the walls."

Olive had smiled, trying to sound casual. "Probably just the wind—or the pipes." But inside, a flicker of curiosity stirred.

Just then, the chimes above the front door jingled, and she set the oatmeal apple cake on a cooling rack.

"Welcome to Annie's—I'll be right with you."

At the same time, her baby kicked into its morning routine. She chuckled.

How can there even be enough room to spread out?

If she had her dates right, she still had a couple of months before their little family grew by one more—another mouth to feed, body to clothe, heart to love.

"No rush, dear! Well, hello, young Simon and Holly."

Mrs. Spagnoletti's singsong voice was unmistakable.

Olive figured her visit likely pertained to rounding up more help for the spring carnival.

Shrugging off the mitts, Olive maneuvered her belly around

the countertop and pushed through the doors—nearly colliding with Carley.

"Hi, Olive—just helping Annie with the catering deliveries."

The young woman, her bright green pixie cut a perfect nod to Saint Patrick's Day, waved to Mrs. S. and the kids before disappearing into the kitchen.

"Olive—just the woman I'm looking for." Mrs. Spagnoletti batted her powder-blue lids.

Uh-oh.

She'd already been tapped for last-minute errands for the carnival. And after church, she'd signed up for a spot at the facepainting station. Annie had also donated cupcakes for the cake walk.

Olive pasted on a smile.

"Can I interest you in a warm slice of oatmeal apple cake and a cup of fresh-brewed caramel pecan?"

Mrs. S.'s eyes sparkled beneath the frosted eyeshadow that had been all the rage back when Olive was in high school. She licked her lips, the vivid pink gloss rivaling the bakery's logo.

"That sounds scrumptious—to go, please." She reached into her large bag and produced a slip of paper. "Here's a list of flavors the cake walk committee agreed on."

Olive took the note—then blinked as she caught sight of the car parked outside.

Her heart stuttered for a half second, expecting Hank's truck, but no—it was Mrs. Spagnoletti's sedan.

Still…something looked off.

A weird slant to the back end? Or maybe it was just the fog and low light playing tricks on her.

She shook it off and patted the older woman's shoulder. "How about I fetch that cake and coffee?"

Without waiting for a response, she slipped through the café doors.

Carley had already rolled out the metal cart they used for catering deliveries. During Annie's predawn call, she'd explained that Finn had kept her up half the night with a nasty cold. And with the fire chief away assisting with hotshot training, Annie had stayed home with their sniffly toddler.

Thank You, Lord, for keeping the children and me healthy.

She flashed back to Pastor Mark's Sunday message about how the Lord's eyes roam the whole earth, looking to encourage those devoted to Him.

Father, forgive me for forgetting how faithfully You see us.

The chimes jingled again, followed by familiar female chatter.

"Hello, ladies!" Mrs. S. trilled. "Olive will be back in a moment."

The kids chimed in their greetings as Olive sliced through the moist cake. A few of her new friends had promised to deep-clean the studio before move-in day.

Still, the car flashed through her thoughts again—something about it didn't sit right.

They still needed Hank to dig out the boxes in the old barn and deliver them to the shop.

And Holly had said something odd the other day—during a quick stop by the bakery after hours, when she'd wandered back toward the kitchen.

"Mommy, I heard a scratchy sound near the heater closet again," she whispered, brow furrowed. "Maybe it's a stowaway—like Coconut on his shipwreck 'ventures."

Olive had brushed it off, chalking it up to wind or creaky ductwork. But with the delay dragging on, she couldn't help wondering if it had been more than a child's imagination—especially when she thought something fluffy had scurried by in her peripheral vision the next time she'd been working, just as a customer distracted her.

And now she couldn't help wondering about something else, too. Because even though she'd tried to quiet her heart, her dreams of a happy ever after hadn't stopped stirring.

After Hank had dropped them off at the ranch that afternoon, she'd finally sat down with the kids.

"But Mom—if Mr. Big isn't our dad, then why're we living here?"

They'd all been perched on the shared bed—Roman stretched across the middle like a stuffed border between real emotions.

Simon's question had nearly undone her.

She'd said a silent prayer, then chosen her words carefully.

"Because Mr. Big generously opened his home for us until we can move into Miss Annie's apartment."

But even as she'd spoken, she'd seen Holly's lower lip tremble, her round eyes fill with tears.

"But we like it here."

So did she.

Not just the cozy warmth of the place or the peace of the quiet land.

But the man behind it all.

Still, all she could do was draw her daughter close and press a kiss to her hair, silently trying to comfort the ache she felt, too.

Because the longer they stayed, the harder it would be to leave.

And the more impossible it felt not to hope for something more.

A burst of laughter from the shop pulled her back to the present. She smoothed her hand over her belly and stepped through the swinging doors.

"Good morning, pretty momma."

Emerson swooped in for a quick hug, her brown eyes sparkling. Miss Marie followed, then Kate.

Lacey had stayed behind at the B and B to serve one of her famous gourmet breakfasts.

"The ladies insisted on playing before working." Miss Marie winked as she tucked a silver strand behind her ear.

Olive smiled in return. "Let me finish up with Mrs. S. and I'll grab us all a snack."

She handed the woman a white bag with the shop's logo and poured a steaming cup of coffee.

As the older woman fluttered her bejeweled fingers and exited, Kate brushed past her.

"You go sit down. I've got this now."

"Well, then." Olive laughed softly and joined her friends, who hovered around Simon and Holly.

Soon, the conversation shifted to the fishing contest—Simon and Holly adding animated commentary.

She figured if they'd lingered after worship, the ladies would've bombarded her with questions then.

But Hank had been called out on a tow. And rather than inconvenience anyone, they'd agreed to ride back to the ranch on his way.

Funny, she'd had second thoughts about letting the kids enter the contest in the first place. But what would she have said, anyway?

She couldn't go back on her promise to let them enter the event. Even if it had forced her to face the swirl of emotions it stirred up.

Especially after watching Hank—a man who admitted to struggling in relationships—in action with her kids.

Nothing short of amazing.

Not to mention how he always flexed his Mr. Fixit muscles without a second thought.

And now she understood him better—why he lay on the overprotectiveness so thick.

His sister's death. His fiancée's desertion.

No wonder he'd shut off his heart.

The two of them weren't so different, really. Both abandoned by people they'd once loved.

"Sorry we haven't had a chance to congratulate you…" Kate grinned as she laid out plates, utensils, and napkins.

Olive arched a brow. What had she missed?

Emerson shot her a mischievous smile as she stood up to help with beverages.

"For the fishing contest win, of course."

Heat bloomed on Olive's cheeks. She toyed with the fraying edge of the napkin resting on her belly.

"The kids had a great time with Hank."

Miss Marie leaned in, voice low, pale eyes twinkling. "I heard they weren't the only ones having fun."

Olive's mouth opened—then closed.

If she denied it, she'd be lying.

Before she could respond, Mrs. Spagnoletti stepped into view outside, her arms full of shopping bags from Main Street.

As she fumbled with her car door, something clicked in Olive's brain—whatever had been niggling at her earlier came into sharp focus.

"Excuse me, ladies." She slid off her chair and maneuvered around the tables as quickly as her belly allowed.

A drizzle met her on the sidewalk, but she barely noticed.

She waved both arms. "Mrs. Spagnoletti!"

The older woman peeked over the top of her car. "What is it, dear—did I forget something?"

Her syrupy sweet perfume hit on a gust of wind, and Olive's stomach lurched.

Still, she breathed a silent prayer of thanks for the supernatural heads-up.

Slightly winded, she slowed her pace as she neared the curb.

"Mrs. Spagnoletti—how long has your rear passenger tire had that bulge?"

The woman closed her door, a crease forming between her brows. She followed Olive's gaze to the tire.

"I really don't know."

"Hank needs to look at it. ASAP."

With a little encouragement, the former councilman's wife agreed to swing by the garage.

Only then did Olive return to the bakery.

The tables were soon cleared and hugs exchanged before the other women headed upstairs with cleaning supplies for the studio.

For a while, Olive kept busy—glancing over the kids' work-sheets between customers.

The phone rang just after she helped a couple from out of town load up on Annie's infamous sweet and sour lemon bars.

"Annie's Confections, Catering & Café, how may I help you?"

"Olive!" Mrs. Spagnoletti's voice held a distinct note of panic. "No one's at the garage—can I come back tomorrow?"

Hank must still be out on a tow.

Olive frowned, explaining gently why the tire couldn't wait.

She'd just promised to meet her at the garage when Kate re-appeared.

The constable's half-sister practically pushed her out the door, promising they'd get the kids to school and hold down the fort till she returned—which was how Olive ended up changing out a damaged tire at seven months pregnant and counting.

If she were honest, she'd half expected Hank to burst into the garage bay with the same frazzled energy he'd had when he thought her water had broken.

The man wouldn't have been happy.

But she needn't have worried.

No sign of her boss.

Breathing a sigh of relief, she closed out the work order.

After changing out of the coveralls, she balled them up for the laundry bin.

Locking up the shop, her thoughts wandered back to the la-dies' mention of the jam session that evening at the B and B.

There was always next week.

But she'd promised the kids. And Holly and Simon contin-ued to thrive here.

Not for the first time, she toyed with the idea of making Sweet-water their forever home—after they fulfilled their Hope House agreement.

She smoothed her hand over her belly.

I still have time to decide.

Scootching behind the wheel of her car, she managed a tired smile.

She'd just prevented a potential tire blowout. Or worse.

Hank couldn't be upset about that.

Could he?

Besides, now that she was driving again—and they'd be out of his hair soon—he was almost scot-free.

Except the tire situation only confirmed what she already knew.

Until his cousin returned to the shop—and the programs she'd helped set up were running on their own—Hank still needed her.

Which had *nothing* to do with how she felt for him.

Olive rolled her eyes as she turned onto Main.

Yeah, right.

Chapter Seven

Olive had stuck around.

Even after Hank had said too much.

Especially that bit about his failed engagement.

Grateful didn't come close to describing her reaction when he'd handed over her car keys.

And she'd fulfilled her temporary arrangement at the garage.

As soon as they were moved out, life would return to normal.

Go ahead, keep telling yourself that.

Was it even possible after the small taste of family life?

He snorted from his spot at the rear of The Lodge.

Not likely. Even if Olive wanted anything to do with a grizzly bear like him, her ex's desertion ran deep—like his.

And she had a thing about not wanting to depend on others.

At least the kids had walked away from the fishing contest with a sweet coffer.

Persh clapped a solid hand on his shoulder.

"How's it goin', Big Country?"

The weekly Wednesday jam session was in full swing, hosted by the Pershings—though tonight's turnout was lighter.

The off-and-on rain had thrown a wrench in more than just his day.

Christian tunes pulsed from the speakers as a local band played its set.

Since Olive still hadn't shown, he'd kept his gaze trained on Simon and Holly, who danced in the aisle with their friends.

His mouth pulled down—and Persh guffawed.

"That good, huh?"

Hand in hand, Charles Bloom and Miss Marie stepped inside, nodding their hellos.

Hank's chest pinched at the sight.

It had taken the widowed pair a long time to find happiness again—proof that the town legend might still have some truth.

Funny how their love story had sparked years earlier on a very different Valentine's Day.

Nothing like the one this year.

He shifted his focus back to the kids, thinking how far they'd come since he'd found them huddled under that evergreen.

A knot of emotion clogged his throat.

I've changed, too.

Maybe that was why he'd struggled loading the Harts' suitcases into the tow truck earlier.

The day had only gone downhill, starting with a multicar pileup.

He'd had to shut down the garage for hours.

Thank You, Lord, for sparing the lives of those involved.

Now the bays were packed again, and the backlog was worse than ever.

Gordie's call had been the one bright spot—he'd found help at his mom's Montana place and, though he'd planned to be gone much longer, would be back as early as next week.

Persh leaned closer, raising his voice over the bass. "I heard that wreck on the interstate was a doozy."

His hazel eyes softened as Lacey slipped in beside him, Ada Mae perched on her hip.

A tsunami of longing hit Hank hard. One he'd long since written off as out of reach.

"That pileup, you mean?"

The sticky humidity had frizzed Lacey's curls and worsened Hank's foul mood.

He nodded. "Thankful my regulars have been patient with the delays—and for the loaners we still had on hand. Except…"

At least Olive's still showing up…but for how long?

"Then it's a good thing our newest resident was available to save the day with the Spagnoletti's sedan," Lacey piped in as she passed Ada Mae to Persh, then kissed her husband's cheek.

Wait…what?

She disappeared into the crowd.

His brain stalled, trying to catch up.

Gobsmacked again.

The last time Mrs. S.'s car had been in the shop was the day Manny quit.

A knowing churned in his gut.

He hadn't logged into the system that afternoon.

"Any clue what—" he started to ask, but his words were swallowed by giggles.

Simon and Holly crashed into him, wrapping around his denim-clad legs.

Everything else faded at their touch.

"Can we play outside, Mr. Big?"

Eyes like Olive's blinked up at him.

He nearly scooped Holly into his arms on instinct—just to hold her close.

Play the superhero she deserved.

Persh bumped his shoulder, grinning. "Catch up with you later, buddy."

Hank crouched to eye level. "Where'd your friends go?"

"Their mommy had a 'mergency at the zoo." A thatch of hair, darker than Olive's, flopped over Simon's eye.

"You mean the preserve and sanctuary—"

What would Jack or Persh do?

"I'm not sure your mommy would want you getting wet."

Still in her rain slicker, Holly dropped her gaze to her boots.

"We've got on boots!"

Hank chuckled. "Well—why didn't you say so?"

He straightened and took their hands. Together, they headed to the exit. The screen door clapped shut behind them.

Twinkle lights cast a soft glow across the yard and gazebo, nestled beside a row of white cottages.

Kids always liked snacks, right?

They could stop at Lacey's spread of appetizers—moved inside now, thanks to the drizzle.

Spring break was right around the corner. Folks had been praying for clearer skies.

Such weird weather lately.

They neared the covered structure—the one that hosted everything from weddings to ladies' Bible study.

The kids tugged him toward it.

Holly broke free and darted into the gazebo, its built-in benches shielding them from the mist.

"Let's play *Shrek*!"

Simon climbed in beside her and looked up. "Yeah, you be the ogre and—"

Hank blinked. The boy had grown like quack grass.

"Me, the ogre? Since when am I green?" He let out a growl. The kids shrieked with laughter.

"Oh—we need a donkey, too!" Holly's smile fell.

Hank scratched at his beard, lifting his eyes skyward. "Well, guys—since Roman's still at the ranch, we'll need a plan B."

Simon scowled and folded his skinny arms tight across his chest. "Don't look at me!"

"What's going on in here?"

Hank startled, eyes snapping to Olive.

How had he missed her approach?

And his reaction was immediate. The cat that Annie rescued last year got his tongue.

Especially as he took in her wild, caramel-colored waves tumbling over her shoulders. A lightweight jacket flapped open to reveal an oversized floral T-shirt skimming dark leggings. Zebra print rainboots—matching her daughter's—finished off the look.

On anyone else? Mismatched.

On Olive? Adorable.

"Mommy!" Holly rushed her with open arms.

Oblivious to his deer-in-the-headlights reaction, Olive scooped both kids into a hug before turning her golden gaze on him.

"What're you guys doing out here?"

"We're playing *Shrek*," Simon said, brushing the unruly shock from his eyes.

"You can play Princess Fiona!"

Holly flashed a gap-toothed smile.

But Olive's gaze never wavered.

He scuffed a boot across the cement. "Emerson had an animal emergency," Hank said, clearing the gravel from his throat.

Memories surfaced—of the infamous llama and alpaca incident a few years back at the preserve. Their deviant antics had become the stuff of legend, somehow bringing together the town's constable and vet with a nudge from Jack's daughter, Josie…and, of course, the resident matchmaker.

"I took over damage control," he added.

Olive seemed satisfied with that. She dropped her bag on a cushion and sank into it. Propping her feet on the short table in the center, she leaned back and shut her eyes.

"Sorry to disappoint, but you're on your own, kids."

"Long day? You look tired," Hank said.

One eye peeled open. She fixed it on him.

Ugh. Not the right thing to say.

Lacey's earlier comment surfaced again.

"Oh, yes—busy at the bakery with Annie out most of the day."

"Huh."

Both eyes opened. She pushed herself upright, arms braced behind her.

He'd said that out loud?

Didn't matter. His gut told him Olive was hiding something.

"It's just… Lacey said something about—"

"Mom, can we get something to eat?" Simon jumped off the bench.

The steady pitter-patter of rain tapped against the gazebo roof, syncing with the easy, jammy chords of bass and string drifting through the yard.

His chest squeezed. "Have you eaten anything?" Whatever Lacey had been getting at could wait.

Olive's head bobbed, lids heavy. "I just want to sit here for a few minutes, is all."

She resettled into the cushions, and within seconds, a soft snore escaped her parted lips.

Hank pressed a finger to his lips and motioned the kids toward the inn.

Accompanied by the light mist, the three of them stepped into the kitchen's cozy warmth.

Lacey had outdone herself again with a generous spread of appetizers on the counter. Hank helped the kids fill their plates, joining a few others grazing.

Mr. Spagnoletti, the former town councilman, lumbered through the swinging café doors and fell in line behind him.

"Big Country!" the man bellowed, clapping him on the back.

Hank glanced over his shoulder. "Good to see you, Mr. S."

"I am forever indebted to your partner for keeping the missus safe today! I mean, if—"

What in blazes is he talking about?

Hank paused, plate halfway filled with fruit. "Sir, I don't know what—"

"Come on, Mr. Big!" Holly yanked on his flannel sleeve, lemon bar crumbs dotting the collar of her jacket.

Still confused, Hank filed the comment away. But the kids were tugging him back toward the gazebo, all three juggling plates stacked with healthy fare, dodging the fat raindrops falling from the sky.

When they stepped inside the wooden structure, Olive opened her eyes, a shy smile curving her lips.

When he handed her a plate—crackers, cheese, salami, straw-berries—his pulse ratcheted and words escaped him.

"Uh—"

"Thank you, Hank."

She grabbed the fork from his hand, and their fingers brushed. Zing.

Their eyes locked. Or maybe it was just him.

But then he remembered.

"Hey, Olive—I heard from a couple folks about your heroism… Care to explain?"

Despite the low light, her eyes darkened.

Just as he suspected.

She waved a hand, rolled her eyes. "It was nothing, really. Bulged tire. Replaced it. Good to go."

But the words didn't slow the simmer in his blood. He arched a brow, waiting.

When she finished recounting her story, only the clink of sil-verware mingling with the soft music and slowing rain remained.

Oh, he had things to say. It took everything in him to keep quiet.

But when he didn't respond, she threw up her hands.

"You weren't at the garage—and there was no way Mrs. S. could drive on that tire, and—"

His hand shook as he ran it over his mussed hair. No use rais-ing a stink in front of the kids.

Still, how could she risk her safety like that?

He pulled in a slow breath and released it like a leaky balloon.

A puff of air passed her lips. "I was going to tell you—even-tually." Her mouth tilted into a saucy pout.

And that's when it hit him.

If Olive hadn't stepped in, Mrs. Spagnoletti's tire could've blown. Could've triggered any number of mechanical issues.

Resignation pooled in his gut. He had no choice but to sell the ranch.

It was the only way.

Expanding the workforce. Increasing the garage's capacity. All necessary. The town had more than doubled in size.

But none of that was the real reason.

The real reason sat across from him, rain-speckled and radiant, eating cheese and strawberries like she wasn't driving him out of his ever-loving mind.

Because there was no telling if Olive would still be around to help.

Especially once he laid down the rules.

"How's your family adjusting to the new living arrangements?"

Emerson joined Olive at one of the round folding tables in the church's multipurpose room.

She and the kids attended morning service after another restless night in the studio apartment.

Since Wednesday's awkward conversation, Hank had helped her move in.

In silence.

Except for the part where he promised to deliver the rest of their belongings stored in his barn.

Compared to the wide-open space of his home, the cramped apartment felt more like a closet with plumbing. And with the rain showing no signs of letting up, the kids had been cooped up inside for days.

Everyone's nerves were wearing thin.

Before she answered, Olive offered another quick prayer for a dry spring break.

"It's been an adjustment, but we're managing," she said finally, keeping her tone light. "Though Simon keeps calling it our rainy day shoebox."

Emerson laughed softly. "He's not wrong."

Olive dabbed her lips with a napkin, and the baby kicked against her belly. "It's just until the baby is born and our Hope House contract is fulfilled."

Emerson studied her face for a moment. "If you need help navigating housing options, I can put out some feelers."

But were they even staying in Sweetwater?

"Thank you. I'll keep that in mind."

Emerson's dark eyes shone with compassion. "Even after renovations to the live-in quarters at the preserve, after Jack and I married and he moved in with Josie and Dewey, it was a tight squeeze."

A burst of laughter drew their attention toward a cluster of kids near the snack table. Holly's curls bounced as she ran to grab a juice pouch, her rain boots squeaking on the polished floor.

Emerson smiled, then glanced over Olive's shoulder. "Oops. I think I'm being summoned."

She gave Olive's hand a gentle pat. "Hang in there."

Then she stood, brushing crumbs from her skirt as another parishioner waved her over—probably with some urgent pet question.

"Back to doctor duty," she said with a wink, then headed across the room.

Olive watched her go, grateful for the support…but still unsettled.

Something about the back room had been bothering her for days—but like so many things this week, it was easier to ignore than address.

She'd just taken a sip of lukewarm coffee when Simon slid into the chair beside her.

"Mom, can I tell you something weird?"

"That depends," she said, warily.

"I keep hearing noises in Miss Annie's kitchen. Like scratching. In the back."

Olive frowned. "In the kitchen or the room off the kitchen?"

"The room, I think." He leaned in. "Holly heard it, too."

Just then, Holly appeared at the table, a mini muffin in one hand and a serious look on her face.

"It's probably a chipmunk."

"A chipmunk?" Olive echoed, curiosity piqued.

"It makes a kind of chirpy sound," Holly explained. "And it's been doing it all week."

That's when Olive recalled the kids' comments she'd brushed off earlier. Before she could respond, Emerson stepped up behind them.

"Did you just say something about a chipmunk?"

"I was going to mention it," Olive admitted, flushing. "There's been some scratching noises in the back utility room off the kitchen. I figured it was the new furnace adjusting, but—"

Emerson gave her a knowing look. "You didn't want to say anything in case it turned out to be nothing."

"Pretty much."

"Well," she said. "I'll swing by tomorrow and take a look. If something's nested in there, better we catch it before it chews through anything important."

Simon looked stricken. "We're not gonna hurt it, right?"

"Not at all," Emerson reassured him. "We'll just find it a better place to live—Jack's been wanting a project for the preserve, anyway."

Olive let her head fall lightly to the table.

From tire changes to chipmunk relocation, this week was filled with a long parade of ridiculous obstacles.

And for some reason, Hank's words in the gazebo still echoed.

"There's gonna be new rules around here…"

She already knew what that meant. First, he'd fallen back into his grizzled ways. Next, he'd relegated her strictly to office tasks.

A harumph escaped her lips. The man had clearly blown her work on Mrs. S.'s tire out of proportion.

"I just wish 'someone' would let me back in the garage," she whispered.

Emerson's perceptive gaze met hers. "I'm going to share a little secret."

The kids had already scampered off, but Emerson leaned in.

"When I first showed up in town, the last thing I wanted was to be ordered around." Her expression turned inward. "I'd just fled an abusive marriage—but the constable's oversize Stetson interjected itself everywhere I turned."

She smirked. "But the man was born to serve and protect—so he told me—and because of the targeted vandalism at the preserve where I lived and worked, well…" Emerson's brown eyes were steady. "He didn't know how to do his job halfway—"

"But—"

Emerson held up a hand. "Early on, Jack told me he and Hank grew up together and he'd observed everything—"

They were interrupted when Jack and Emerson's children skipped to the table—Holly and Simon on their heels.

"Are we going to the preserve soon, Mom?"

Josie's white-blond braid matched her mother's dark one in style if not in color. Her pretty, bright blue eyes mirrored her biological father's, while Anthony, though adopted, had tan skin that favored Emerson.

She winked at the kids. "If the rain lets up—or we might stop at the bakery for a treat."

Loud cheers trailed behind as the four of them scampered across the floor.

Emerson had invited Holly and Simon to join their family—a thoughtful way to give Olive a reprieve.

But how to fill the hours?

Upkeep in the studio took a fraction of the time compared to the roomy ranch.

Her focus shifted back to the woman next to her. "Hank told me about what happened with his ex," she said.

In fact, his grisliness had resurfaced not long after.

Emerson shook her head. "I'm talking about his sister—Rosie."

Olive's chest constricted. "Car wreck, right?" Though she knew little else.

"Yes—though it might've been prevented." Emerson's gaze

softened. "If a headstrong teenager had heeded her older brother's warnings."

She paused, took a sip of water. "A blizzard—much like the one you'd been caught in—hit town. Hank told her she couldn't use his car to meet her boyfriend."

Annie, too, had mentioned a winter storm the night Hank came to their aid.

Pastor Mark stepped up to their table just then.

"Hi, ladies—sorry to interrupt."

After a quick update on the spring carnival, Emerson picked up their conversation.

"But Rosie took Hank's car anyway." She pursed her lips. "She drove on bald tires—he'd been waiting for the cash to pay for replacements."

Returning the glass to the table, Emerson folded her hands.

"He woke up in the middle of the night and just knew—"

Olive stifled a gasp and pressed her fingers to her lips.

Absently, she reached for the water next to her.

Instead of the telltale sweetness she'd grown used to, fresh cucumber coated her tongue.

She swallowed—the cool beverage pushing past the lump in her throat.

"What happened next?"

So engrossed in Emerson's account of that fateful night that marked Hank's life, Olive had tuned out everything but the woman's words and downcast gaze.

"At the time, Jack was a newbie officer—and first responder at the scene."

The blame Hank must live with every day since.

The noble pursuit to fix everything in his power. Pushing away his fiancée. Sabotaging future relationships.

A draft brushed past her as she shifted in her chair. She thought back to that day in the bakery's kitchen after Hank checked out the broken-down furnace. He hadn't mentioned critters or causes to Annie, but the way he'd carried himself made her wonder if there was more beneath the surface.

Now, in light of the scratching sounds in the back room, she couldn't help but feel Hank's surliness was its own brand of concern.

That's when her heart skipped a beat—sudden understanding washing over her.

He cares for me.

From the sparkle in Emerson's eyes, she realized her friend had beaten her to the punch.

But Donny's desertion had hit Olive hard. She'd vowed not to allow another man into her life.

She had Holly and Simon to think about, after all.

And despite Granddad's assurances, history had only confirmed she was more trouble than she was worth.

Hank's reaction to Mrs. S.'s tire proved it.

What did I do to deserve a burden like you?

The horrible words her mother once spoke to her filtered into her subconscious.

A quiet nudge stirred in her heart—a sense that she needed to hand over her worries.

An unfurling in her spirit nearly took her breath away. But it wouldn't come easy. Could she learn how?

She sat in the silence, absorbing the tragic story Emerson had shared.

"Last call!"

One of the parishioners hollered from the kitchen, and an idea struck.

She could start with something small.

Finally, the clouds had lifted—literally and figuratively. Olive's spirits soared beneath the blue skies while she drove down the interstate.

Patches of snow still lingered in the forest where the sun didn't reach.

As she passed the pullout area where her family had gone off the road, she realized her hands no longer sweat.

Still, she kept an eye out for stray animals—a niggle of apprehension shooting down her spine at the thought of Hank's sister losing control on a road much like this one.

Emerson had opened her eyes to Hank's tragic past—convincing Olive to meet the mechanic halfway.

She glanced at the cooler beside her.

It may have been a small step toward learning to lay her burdens at God's feet, but it was something. A small gesture that might help mend things after going over her boss's head.

Her hand strayed to her belly. Only in hindsight had she realized how foolish she'd been. Changing Mrs. S.'s tire had been a risk she couldn't afford to take.

Thank You, Lord, for protecting the unwary—and for second chances.

She flicked on her turn signal. As the tires crunched over the gravel, she thought back to the first night Hank had brought them here.

Funny how much could change in a short time.

And how much she missed this place.

After the potluck, the cleanup crew had nearly shoved her out of the kitchen. But not before she packed up leftovers for Hank.

He hadn't been at the garage when she stopped by earlier. Just a ragged scrap of paper taped to the door.

OUT ON A TOW.

"Okay, plan B, then."

And now here she was, still in the knit green dress a parishioner had dropped off that first Sunday, headed toward a ranch house that had come to mean far more than she ever expected.

Warmth bloomed in her chest at the thought of that first welcoming committee.

Maybe, just maybe, she could build something here—once she fulfilled her Hope House commitment.

But would Hank keep her on at the garage?

She'd walked into Hank & Gordie's, not knowing what her future held. Annie wouldn't be required to house or employ her after the baby came. And yet every day, Sweetwater felt more like a sanctuary.

Even Emerson had shared a similar story of seeking refuge here.

The ranch came into view—more of a home than the one she'd shared with Donny. And all those feelings? The ones she'd been stuffing down? They came barreling back, stirred by the man who lived here.

"Stop it," she whispered aloud.

For thou hast been a refuge from the storm.

The verse struck her heart—a reminder of God's hand on that blizzardy Valentine's night.

Maybe a nudge to believe the promises in Granddad's Bible.

She pictured Hank's ruddy cheeks, those kind blue eyes—when he wasn't acting all Hank the Crank. She cracked a smile, then sobered.

"Lord, the last thing I'm looking for is a replacement for Donny."

Not that Donny was even in the same league.

She parked and shook her head. Now was not the time for schoolgirl fantasies—not when his gruffness was clearly a wall guarding something deeply broken. And he hadn't yet figured out she wasn't worth his time. Or maybe he still saw her as a rescue project.

She grabbed the cooler and stepped out. After dropping off the food, she'd check on the rest of their belongings in the barn—save Hank the trouble.

Roman wasn't around, but she half expected to hear the jingle of his tags.

Inside, she swung through the kitchen and then out the sliding glass door. Mud sucked at her shoes as she followed the path toward the barn, heart tightening at the memory of suggesting they convert it into an event space.

Not that Hank had been too keen on that.

As she stepped inside, the storage area came into view—and her heart plummeted straight to her swollen ankles.

She froze.

"Oh no."

Boxes on pallets had been torn into. Mold climbed the cardboard. Holes chewed through bags, leaving a ruined mess of what had once been her family's keepsakes.

"Olive?"

She whirled around, hand to her chest.

Hank stood in the doorway, shoulders broad, blue eyes wide and concerned. His gaze swept the room and landed on the damage.

Without a word, they each opened boxes.

Mildew clung to baby books. Rodents had torn through Holly's toddler scribbles.

Hank swiped at his beard. "Well, I'll be a fish on a hook."

He looked up at the ceiling, jaw tight. "Rain and rodents. Quite the welcoming party."

Then he stepped toward her.

And she didn't think—just folded herself into his arms.

He smelled like grease—and home.

"I'm so sorry," he whispered, his hand rubbing slow circles on her back.

Something deeper rang in his tone. Like maybe the apology went beyond the barn.

Maybe it was for every gruff moment that meant he cared more than he let on.

And just like that, panic hit. They were too close.

She stepped back abruptly, smoothing the dress and averting her gaze.

So much was gone. Irreplaceable.

God, I feel so defeated.

"Come on," Hank said gently. "Let's get inside."

He kept a respectful distance as they walked back to the house.

"Someone dropped off so much food, it'll take a herculean effort to make a dent."

He winked.

She smiled despite herself.

"Then we'll figure out if anything can be saved," Hank said.

But how would she break this news to the kids?

They'd been so strong—until the move to the studio. She knew they missed this place, too.

Had moving to Sweetwater been just another mistake in a long line?

Once more, a gentle stirring in her spirit reminded her He would make a way, step by step.

"And after that," Hank added, "maybe you'd like to return to the shop?"

She blinked. "You mean—back at the garage?"

He nodded, the corner of his mouth lifting. "Only if you're up to it."

Her heart swelled at his offer. Still, time was running out. The baby would be here soon, and she had just enough saved for a small down payment somewhere. But she already knew where Simon and Holly would pick—and if she were honest? So would she.

As Hank opened the door and stepped through, she followed, feeling the echo of two hearts pounding in rhythm.

It had just been a temporary arrangement, she reminded herself. Nothing more. The timing was all wrong.

If only her own heart had gotten the message.

Chapter Eight

Only a few minutes left on the clock.

Olive brushed a curl off her forehead. She was beyond ready to lock up the bakery, having been on her feet a bit more after helping plan an event last week.

Annie and a few staff members had left hours earlier to cater a gathering at the firehouse.

Right on cue, a pair of munchkins—radars attuned to her thoughts—plowed through the kitchen door, letting it slam on its hinges.

"Hi, Mom!"

Holly and Simon burst into the bakery, their faces flushed from play.

At least they'd left Roman in the backyard.

Olive dropped the rag she'd been using to wipe down the high-top tables and scooped both kids into her arms.

Her heart swelled with gratitude.

According to the weather forecast, a dry spring break was expected. A blessing.

Holly wriggled from Olive's hug and swiped at the honey-tinted bangs tumbling across her eyes.

"Josie said there's a *fun-raiser* at the firehouse tonight—can we go?"

At the sound of Holly's voice, the baby gave a gentle kick.

Olive rested a hand on her belly, heart tugged by the sweetness of both the moment and her daughter's mispronunciation, but even that didn't stop her spirits from dipping.

All week, the town buzzed about the dinner hosted by the fire department. And for good reason—it would raise funds for the Hot Mommas, the nonprofit Annie and Josh had launched.

"Everybody's gonna be there!" Simon's excitement was contagious. "They're having s'ghetti!"

But all Olive wanted was to kick off her sneakers and elevate her swollen feet in their tiny apartment.

Better yet—hibernate until the spring carnival next weekend.

But the kids had been stuck inside too much lately.

And the fundraiser *was* for a good cause.

According to Annie, the reserves were earmarked to help any staff member facing personal setbacks.

The Hot Mommas was formed after one of their own—Billy Charter—took an extended leave to care for his sick wife and their five children.

An eager set of eyes tugged at Olive's heartstrings.

She arched her back with a wince. "Is Roman still out back?"

"We took him back upstairs, Mom. So, can we go?"

She ruffled Simon's thick hair—already in need of another trim. Soon, he'd need new shoes, too.

The bells over the door jingled just then. Her pulse trilled.

She caught herself. Expectant of Hank's arrival.

After discovering their damaged belongings in his shed, things had returned to a comfortable camaraderie—and he'd even invited her back to help on the garage floor.

But once he no longer needed her help—or she went into labor—she suspected their temporary arrangement would end.

After all, Gordie had come home.

His appearance was a sharp contrast to his cousin's—slim build, long white ponytail, and two-plus decades his senior etched into the lines of his skin.

Except his hands-on presence was likely short-lived—if he truly meant what he said about taking a silent role in the business.

So most of her time at Hank & Gordie's was now spent wrapping up the internship details before her due date.

Unconsciously, she rested her hand on her belly.

At least she hadn't started nesting.

Fighting the weariness pressing on her shoulders, she forced a smile and turned toward the new arrival.

"Welcome to Annie's Confections, Catering & Café."

A stylish man in his mid-forties flashed a grin almost too white. A hawkish nose preceded him as he raked manicured fingers through his dark hair.

"Ma'am." He nodded, his eyes dropping to her midsection—where her apron stretched taut.

She squirmed beneath his smarmy inspection and cleared her throat.

Beady eyes snapped to hers.

"Kids—run along and fetch Roman. Wait for me in the yard."

"Yippee!" Holly and Simon shouted, already scampering for the door.

Before she could change her mind, they were gone.

Lord, let this transaction go quickly.

She pasted on a smile. "Let me guess—"

He stepped closer, and her insides shuddered.

What was it about the man that rattled her?

"You made the trip to Sweetwater for our infamous sweet and sour lemon bars."

She waved toward the confections behind the glass.

Still, uneasiness slithered up her spine.

He flashed that blinding grin again. "Let's make it two—since I'm celebrating."

He loosened his tie and popped two buttons at his collar.

Olive quickly donned gloves and retrieved the remaining bars from the shelf, sneaking a few glances at the stranger.

Trying to place him.

"Oh?"

After ringing up his purchase at the old-fashioned register, she handed him a white bag stamped with the bakery's bright pink logo.

Slick leaned in. Stale smoke clung to his expensive clothing.

"You didn't hear it from me, miss—but this Podunk town's economy is about to skyrocket." He rubbed his palms together—like a spider preparing to spin its web. But unlike Charlotte, this one wasn't weaving anything good.

She hitched an eyebrow, inviting him to continue.

"Thanks to the deal I all but signed with Mr. Valentine."

Her hand flew to her chest.

A bitter taste coated her mouth at the sound of Hank's surname rolling off Slick's tongue.

What was he talking about?

She couldn't help recalling Lacey's condensed version of the unscrupulous developer who'd once planned to turn historic Main Street into a strip mall.

"Oh, I see." Though she didn't.

"Yes, ma'am." He glanced over his shoulder, then turned back, a smug expression inching across his narrow face. "Once Cartwright Realty and All American Auto show up on the scene, there'll be no stopping the businesses clambering to set up shop."

He plucked the bag from her hand, winked, then pivoted on leather soles that reeked of wealth.

The bells jingled overhead—a cheerful contrast to the drumroll pounding in her ears.

What deal had he made with Hank? Because a decade ago, All American Auto took her hometown by storm.

Instead of helping the community as promised, mom-and-pop shops had been put out of business.

Would that happen here?

It's none of my business what Hank does with his garage.

But once she delivered the baby and her Hope House arrangement ended, she'd still need a job.

Even if Hank kept her on, All American was notorious for bringing in its own staff.

The back door banged open, snapping her out of her thoughts. "Mom, are you coming?"

"Just a few more minutes," she said, waving them toward the yard.

A half hour later, the four of them piled into the SUV.

But her encounter with the oily stranger continued to needle her.

She found a parking spot near the firehouse and locked up, her hopes pinned on gleaning enough gossip that evening to figure out Hank's plans.

Up ahead, Roman trotted down the sidewalk, tail wagging—Holly and Simon trading off on his leash.

Olive let herself relax, just a little, her eyes drifting to the trees beginning to bud despite nighttime temps that still dipped below freezing.

Much like Snowpeak, March in Sweetwater was known for its wet springs.

They arrived at the firehouse—overflow parking already full. The kids raced ahead to join the growing crowd.

A buffet table stretched across the largest bay, the air rich with the spicy scent of Annie's Italian marinara.

Round portable tables were arranged in the center of the space. Then she saw it.

This was no ordinary fundraiser.

Pastel-hued balloons and streamers transformed the firehouse into a nursery, complete with giant cardboard cutouts of baby bottles, rattles, and blocks.

Stacked on a table near the shiny red fire engine, multicolored paper and ribbons decorated packages of all sizes.

"Olive—you're here!"

Annie's topknot bobbed toward her, a pregnancy glow brightening her round cheeks. She pushed up black frames, then clasped Olive's hands.

"Please don't be upset..." She searched her face. "But when

Hank told us about what happened to your things…" She sighed. "I mean, nothing can replace the mementos, but—"

Hank did this? For me? For us?

Her lips parted, eyes stinging as she blinked, her chest tightening.

"I know you don't like a fuss, but he wanted it to be a surprise."

Annie's arm settled around her shoulders. "Now, let's get you something to eat."

Still reeling, Olive let her guide her toward the buffet.

All the while, she scanned the crowd for the man behind the evening.

Familiar and new faces greeted her as the combination fundraiser–baby shower got underway.

Unused to being the center of attention, a warm flush crept along her neckline.

It was too much. How would she ever repay the added kindness?

This question lingered long after Annie ducked away to check on her caterers—and while Olive helped Holly and Simon load up their plates.

She settled them at a table where Roman curled up beneath their feet, then made her way back to the food line.

The rich baritone voice of Fire Chief Josh boomed from the station's loudspeakers.

"Thank you to everyone who donated to the Hot Mommas—"

He lifted a hand, pausing until the crowd quieted.

"Managed by my very own hot momma—"

Laughter rolled through the group.

His gaze found Annie, standing to the side with eighteen-month-old Finn propped on her hip. The love in his expression made Olive's throat tighten.

Gaze lingering on his wife, he turned back to the crowd.

"And thank you for celebrating the pending arrival of our newest resident's baby."

Heads turned.

Olive gulped, the spotlight singeing her skin.

Then a large hand—rough, steady, and familiar—gently plucked the plate from her grasp.

"Allow me."

Hank's gruff voice sent a jolt up her spine. His arm brushed hers, and a trail of tingles danced across her bare skin.

She shook off the reaction, blaming her sudden gooseflesh on the cooling evening air.

He moved down the food line, adding greens, pasta, meat sauce, and a slab of focaccia to the plate. She murmured her thanks—only to spot Lacey Pershing nearby.

Ada Mae clung to her mother's long skirt, but Lacey's rapt gaze set off silent alarm bells.

Oh, no, you don't.

Instead of the pitchers filled with what she assumed was the inn's proprietary brew, Olive bypassed them and ladled herself some punch.

She'd meant to thank Hank for being so thoughtful.

But the moment passed, swallowed by the delicious meal, conversation about the spring carnival, and the start of gift opening beneath strokes of muted fuchsia, tangerine, and gold in the sky.

For the most part, she'd managed to deflect the questions about her plans after the baby was born—mainly because she still hadn't made any.

"Are you feeling okay?"

As if he sensed her drift toward heavier thoughts, Hank shifted.

She glanced toward the kids—Simon and Holly giggling on the fire engine with their friends while Chad Harrington, one of the station's firefighters, supervised.

Still, she shivered beneath the waning light, even with several propane heaters stationed nearby.

"You're cold."

Without waiting, Hank shrugged out of his flannel shirt. His

T-shirt stretched across broad shoulders and arms that looked like they could bench-press the fire truck.

She dropped her gaze as he draped the warm flannel around her shoulders.

The scent—pungent oil and grease—stirred a deep ache for Granddad. Her rock. The one person who'd never let her down.

After Donny. After her mom. After a lifetime of letting herself believe she was too much for anyone to stick around.

Why was it so hard to accept help?

"I can't keep all this."

She motioned toward the pile of gifts—boxes and bags that would fill up half her apartment.

Her eyes drifted over the whitewashed bassinette, stacks of tiny onesies, newborn teething rings, nursing bottles, and children's books.

Her favorite gift, by far? The crocheted blanket Emerson had made—soft yellow, spring green, and orange. A rainbow of welcome.

Hank's brows furrowed as he scratched his chin.

"I don't understand—"

She laid a hand on his forearm. Beneath her fingers, his pulse stuttered.

"You need to stop trying to fix my problems." Her voice dropped. "I'll never be able to repay everyone."

She wasn't talking about gifts anymore. She was talking about everything—every time she hadn't measured up. Every time love had to be earned, and she came up short.

"Olive."

Hank's palm dwarfed hers, his gaze searching.

"This is how it works around here. People give because they care. No strings."

His expression softened. "Besides, it was my fault your stuff got ruined."

Before she could answer, movement caught her attention.

A tall figure lingered near the curb, mostly hidden in the shadows. Her stomach dipped.

She thought of Slick's visit to the bakery and how Hank's jaw tightened whenever the ranch was mentioned.

"You're selling your ranch?"

He gave a small nod. "Still prayin' about it."

From behind them, a small voice rose above the chatter.

"Mr. Big! Got any fish jokes?"

Holly climbed onto Hank's lap as if it were the most natural thing in the world. Her eyes squeezed shut, and she giggled when his coarse beard tickled her neck.

Olive's heart squeezed at the sweet moment.

Then the giant teddy bear leaned closer to her daughter and whispered conspiratorially, "Do you know what kind of fish you see in the air after a rainstorm?"

Holly shook her head—dark blond hair spilling over her cheeks.

Simon skidded next to Hank, face flushed. "I know—a rainbow trout!"

Hank tossed back his head and chuckled, his smile as wide as her son's puffed-out chest.

"Are we still goin' to the 'reserve next week?"

"Excuse me?" Olive lifted a brow.

Hank might not realize it, but their conversation about the ranch—and her visit from the Cartwright Realty rep—wasn't over.

But what was this about a trip to the wildlife sanctuary?

Three sets of eyes locked on hers.

A sheepish smirk tugged at the corners of Hank's ruddy face. "I might have mentioned something about hitting the preserve on the first day of spring."

"Can we, Mom—pretty please?" Simon bounced on his toes, his earnest plea tugging at her resolve.

Hank lifted his hand. "Of course—their mother is invited, too."

He absently dropped his hand to Roman's head and stroked his pointy ears, but she caught the flicker of hope in his gaze.

It mirrored the ache she woke to each morning.

After Donny's desertion, she'd asked the Lord to bring a father figure into her kids' lives.

Over the past month, Hank had filled that role in ways that scared her.

Had even made her start to believe in answered prayers—for herself.

Companionship. A strong man to lean on.

She swallowed and glanced toward the remaining guests lingering by the refreshment table.

The final notes of a baby shower her boss had set into motion.

Turning back to Hank, she offered him a soft smile. "What time should we meet you there?"

He grinned just as Simon punched the air with a triumphant fist.

"I'll pick everyone up after school."

"You're the best, Mom!"

Holly slid off Hank's lap and gave Olive a quick hug before running off with Simon to share the news with their friends.

She'd only agreed because it was the perfect opportunity to convince Hank not to sell the ranch.

It wasn't in his best interest. Or the town's.

Or hers.

Because it would only dash the hopes she didn't dare entertain.

Time was funny.

Hank double-checked the specifications on the spark plug he'd just torqued.

Gordie had been back a week or so now, yet it was as if the man had never left.

Not if you considered the easy way they'd fallen back into their old rhythm—the easy banter, the shared love of all things with gears and grease.

"So ya' think this Cartwright fellow is on the up and up?"

Gordie peered over the hood of Kate's SUV, gray eyes still sharp.

Hank never gave his cousin's age a second thought—but he noticed the new stoop to Gordie's shoulders. The deep grooves carved into his gaunt face.

The toll of caring for his ailing mother and running a working ranch in Western Montana.

Slouched against the passenger door, eighteen-year-old Angel— a mentee from The Lodge—listened quietly.

Raised by a single mom, the teen was a beneficiary of the Pershings' nonprofit and came highly recommended by the councilman.

Hank straightened from the Range Rover he'd been working on and shoved a rag into his back pocket.

For reasons he couldn't quite pin down, Gordie's question only watered the seeds of doubt Olive's inquiry about the sale had planted.

"He appears to be," he said, thinking back to the realtor's enthusiasm, which had bolstered his decision.

"He plans to overhaul the whole property."

He pointed at Gordie and smirked. "Just think—the proceeds I invest will ultimately be payin' for your retirement."

They laughed.

But the truth was, Hank meant it. It was the least he could do.

His cousin had saved him. After the unexpected deaths of his parents. His sister's tragic accident.

It had been Gordie who brought him on at the garage from day one. Who led him back to the Lord—

Gordie leaned in to speak to Angel, and together they watched the teen shuffle out of the bay.

When it was just the two of them, Gordie turned to him.

"What about Ms. Hart?"

And there it was, the million-dollar question.

"What about her?"

Hank shifted his attention to the pickup next in line.

One minute, he was playing Shrek for the Hart kids. The next, he'd been near paralyzed at the thought of Olive changing Mrs. S.'s tire while pregnant.

Instead of facing his emotions like a bison facing a storm, he'd run from them.

Kept himself busy. Organized a baby shower. Promised the kids an outing.

He tugged on his beard, fidgeting under his cousin's watchful gaze.

"That was a nice thing you did for the Harts." Gordie tossed his ponytail over his shoulder.

And by the look on his face, Hank knew he wasn't done.

"If I'm not mistaken…seems Mr. Fixit is back—"

Hank gave a hard shake of his head.

Okay, it started that way.

That was no excuse for the chip on his shoulder. The one that had settled in after he dropped off the Harts' suitcases.

Returned to his tomblike house—an empty shell that matched his heart. And his track record of failures.

He shrugged, brushing off Gordie's comment with feigned nonchalance.

"It was my fault for stowing their stuff in the storage room."

He winced. The excuse had sounded better in his thick skull.

Still, against his better judgment, he'd invited Olive back to work in the bays.

She had a way with engines, he'd argued. And the shop had never run better.

Didn't hurt that she smelled good, too.

He snorted.

Yet he couldn't shake a sense of duty to prove the woman wrong.

She felt unworthy. Unlovable.

"Isn't that what you think of yourself?"

Hank jerked.

Gordie's words slammed into his gut—just as Angel returned to the bay.

"What now, boss?"

Had he said that part out loud? Voiced his thoughts about Olive's insecurities?

Is that my problem, God?

Though he blamed himself for his sister's death, he'd never viewed his attempts at retribution the same way.

"Never mind, coz."

Gordie gave Angel's bony shoulders a firm squeeze. "You did a great job on Kate's car, young man. Meet me out front, and we'll close out the work order."

Then he turned back to Hank. Compassion and brotherly love shone from his pale eyes.

"Promise me you'll seek God's plans for the ranch first—okay?"

Hank fished the Cartwright rep's business card from his wallet.

He's right, Lord. Show me Your plan.

Hank nodded, then stuffed the card into his pocket.

"Okay—so what're you still doing here?" Gordie arched his silver brows. "Didn't you say something about an outing with the Harts?"

The reminder lit a fire under his feet.

He would pray on Cartwright's offer.

But he wasn't about to break another promise to Olive or the kids.

It's not a date, though.

He just liked hanging out with Simon and Holly.

Same as he would with any other friends.

Pivoting on his heel, he made a beeline for his makeshift apartment to change out of his work clothes.

Keep telling yourself that, Valentine.

A refrain he repeated—all the way to the bakery and while helping Olive and company into the tow truck.

Still, he couldn't ignore how his heart picked up around them; how it beat to a lighter rhythm since that snowy Valentine's Day.

"Mr. Big, why is Petey doing that?"

Holly pointed to a peacock mid-strut, his sapphire feathers fanned into full display.

A rattling sound followed his slow, deliberate circle in front of the admiring crowd.

All five of them—including Roman—had stopped to watch Petey show off.

The peacock had stolen the show. And he knew it.

Beside Hank, Olive stifled an unladylike snort.

He scrunched up his forehead and peeked at her over his shoulder.

It was a balmy spring afternoon for the books.

Her thick caramel-tinted hair hung in loose braids, framing her makeup-free face.

A fresh reminder that several years separated them. Still, she smirked.

A challenge?

Game on.

He turned his full attention to Holly—her round eyes wide with curiosity.

"Well, you see, Miss Holly—Petey there is tryin' to get himself a date."

Olive sputtered as Holly's lips formed a round, silent O.

"Is that what you do, too?"

Next to his sister, Simon flashed a knowing smile—wiser than his years.

Hank's collar tightened as he gulped.

"Um—with peacocks, they—"

"Oh, boy," Olive muttered under her breath. She casually rested one hand on her belly, then nodded toward the next exhibit.

"Kids, that's not how God made humans."

"Coco!"

Both kids tore off toward a wooden fence, Petey forgotten.

"No climbing!" She sighed as Simon and Holly released their grip on the enclosure railing.

It housed Coconut the chimpanzee—a recent addition to the preserve.

"Smart call," Hank said.

The two of them took their time catching up.

Olive's subtle floral scent reminded him of the colorful arrangements Charles Bloom sold in his shop.

She released a soft chuckle. "Sometimes I wonder how I'll keep up with those two after the baby's born."

She had to be joking. Instead of the bright pink coveralls like she wore at the garage, she deserved a cape.

"Emerson told me about Josie's sprained wrist a few years back," she said.

He felt the weight of her gaze. Tugged on his collar.

A chipmunk darted past, pausing long enough to flick its tail at them.

A welcome diversion.

Hank pointed. "Hey—speakin' of Emerson, she mentioned rehoming that little stowaway to the preserve."

Olive squinted at the critter. "You think that's Chip?"

Hank shook his head with a grin, thinking of all the tiny signs the kids had noticed. "Wouldn't surprise me. Looked pretty smug pokin' his head through the hole he chewed in the wall before Doc showed up, didn't he?"

Olive laughed, and something in his chest gave way.

He chuckled again, remembering the kids squealing as they chased the tiny furball—and Olive giggling so hard she nearly doubled over. Relief had washed through him then. He'd noticed the wood shavings near the furnace vent and the faint chittering in the walls. He hadn't wanted to trouble Annie and had forgotten to mention it to Josh. But seeing that little chipmunk scurrying across the floor made it clear: the breakdown hadn't been vandalism.

"So—do you ever ask out the ladies?"

Where had that come from?

"Wha—huh?" he stammered, near about choking on his tongue.

Slowly, he turned from Coco's antics and met Olive's golden gaze, brimming with mischief.

"You could say I'm a bit rusty."

When was the last time he'd dated anyone? Back when Emerson had helped him brush up on skating. Two dates with the woman he'd been trying to impress were all it took before he scared her off—all that badgering about car safety.

Olive kept her eyes on the kids as they tried to get Coco's attention.

"What about you?" Hank coughed against the back of his hand.

Was he crossing a line?

"You and your ex must've shared something special—"

He turned toward Holly and Simon—just in time to catch the shadow that clouded Olive's eyes.

The tell. She'd heard him.

A few seconds ticked by.

She lightly rested her hands on the fence and faced him.

"Except for Granddad, Donny was the first person who ever made me feel seen, and—"

Longing tugged at her lips. His eyes dipped with a mind of their own.

"Special," she finished on a sigh.

A sigh that buried itself beneath his skin—every nerve standing on end.

Or maybe it was the golden streaks in her hair, highlighted by the sun's rays.

His gaze snapped to hers.

Without thinking, he covered her hand with his—just as the kids tore off toward the petting zoo.

He expected her to follow, but her eyes had locked on their joined hands, his dwarfing hers.

Made him feel like a protector.

Her pulse fluttered beneath his palm, and he swallowed. "You are, you know."

She smirked. "Thank you, Hank. Apparently, I wasn't the only parishioner who heard Pastor Mark preach on how fearfully and wonderfully God made us."

Coco blew a raspberry from his perch, and they both chuckled.

"I think he's trying to tell us it's time to get movin'."

She started to slip from his grasp.

Without a second thought, he threaded his fingers through hers.

A tiny tremor passed between them as they followed the kids to the duck enclosure in comfortable silence.

Holly and Simon dodged the fowl, then moved to Louie and Alvin's pen.

His heart had been trying to do the same. To dodge what he'd known all along.

This. It's what he wanted.

The whole package, Lord.

As if she sensed the direction of his thoughts, Olive peeked at him through thick lashes.

Time standing still wasn't just a silly cliché.

His gaze dropped to the pulse fluttering against her smooth neck. Only one step closer to filling the gap, and—

"Mom! Mr. Big!"

Holly and Simon sprinted toward them, swiping at their shirts.

"The llama spit all over us!" Their shrieks carried equal parts horror and fascination. And dispelled whatever might've happened.

Olive released his hand, focus shifting to the kids.

Cold. That's how he felt without the warmth of her skin against his.

The moment had passed. Which was probably a good thing.

Especially when his gaze shifted behind him.

Persh—Ada Mae riding high on his shoulders—nodded at him with a knowing look.

A reminder to keep his head on straight. Not to entertain a future with the Harts.

Not when the rep from Cartwright kept hounding him for an answer.

And the future of the garage was at stake.

"All clean—now run along."

Olive tucked a bottle of hand sanitizer in her bag, and the kids scooted off to visit Pearl the potbellied pig, Roman trotting behind them on his leash.

"Llama spit cooties averted," she joked.

And when he looked into her sparkling eyes, he forgot everything he'd just told himself.

"So the spring carnival on Saturday…" He shoved his shaking hands into his pockets. "I… uh… I was wondering if you'd like to go. With me."

Her peach-tinted lips parted as she studied his face.

"Oh—you mean a date?" She giggled.

He coughed, brows lifting. "Yes. A date."

A gentle smile puckered the skin around her eyes, dancing with glee.

"Should I be insulted you didn't display Petey fanfare?"

He chuckled, exhaling a breath he hadn't realized he'd been holding.

"And… I'd like that." A flush pinked her cheeks. "As long as Mrs. S. doesn't come looking for us."

Her smile was everything.

She swatted his bicep and fell into step beside him, their arms brushing.

He had a date!

With three chaperones.

That should've calmed his nerves.

But later that day—beneath the midnight blue sky, surrounded by the stillness of his family ranch—the words Simon had whispered to him came rushing back.

An innocent question, spoken when he'd dropped the Harts off at the bakery.

"Do you like our mom?"

It had pierced a hole in his daydreams.

Replaced them with a question. One that had dodged his boots since Olive—her whole family—stormed into his life.

"What if I scare them away?" he'd whispered into the quiet, seeking the Lord's counsel.

In the cloak of night, a coyote answered with a lonely howl.

But what if he didn't?

Still…would she stay once the baby was born?

He'd overheard her at the baby shower, her quiet uncertainty about what came next.

And as he picked his way back to the house, he was certain of one thing.

He liked the children's mother.

A lot.

How he felt around her. The kids.

Even if he hadn't factored a family into his long-range plans.

Before bed—business far from his mind—he rifled through stacks of slacks and rumpled shirts in his closet.

Right now, he had more pressing matters.

What to wear to the spring carnival.

Chapter Nine

Spring break had zipped by.

Only five more weeks until her due date, confirmed by her obstetrician that week.

But her doctor's parting words had done a number on the applecart.

There was still so much she wanted to get done.

"It's time to get off your feet, momma."

The physician—close to Olive's age—had patted her shoulder. "Before the decision is made for you."

Ouch.

After the spring carnival, she'd whispered to herself at the time.

She removed a pan of sweet and sour lemon bars from the oven now.

Thoughts of the wildlife sanctuary outing brought heat to her cheeks.

A simple invitation from Hank had turned into so much more.

Farm-fresh fragrance. Springtime growth. Squawks and chirps drifting from the aviary exhibit.

The quiet ease between her and Hank.

The spark of anticipation.

Until Louie the llama spit at both kids—triggering full-blown meltdowns.

Still, she'd caught the hope in Hank's eyes. Felt his pulse where their palms touched.

Something had shifted. And now they had a date on Saturday.

But none of her maternity clothes fit the bill.

And the closest malls were hours away.

She'd been eyeing a pair of cowgirl boots in one of Sweetwater's upscale boutiques.

Maybe she could splurge—just a little. She still had a few dollars tucked away after her doctor's appointment. Granddad had called it "mad money."

She peeled off the oven mitts as the bells over the bakery door jingled.

She'd already received a dozen texts from Mrs. S. about carnival prep, so when it was Kate who pushed through the swinging doors, a sigh escaped her lips.

"Olive! I was hoping to catch you."

Her icy blue eyes—so much like Jack's—sparkled as she pulled her into a quick hug.

"How's Momma and baby?"

Kate fluffed her dark, shoulder-length hair, but not before Olive caught a flicker of something wistful in her expression.

When Olive first arrived, she'd heard hushed whispers about Kate's difficult past—her quiet divorce, the shocking family secrets, and a search for her only living relative, the constable.

Not long afterward, she'd moved to Sweetwater to start over. Found family in the community.

Something Olive was learning to recognize, too.

"Kate—what a pleasant surprise," she said, tucking a strand of hair into her ponytail. "What can I offer you?"

The part-time journalist smoothed a hand over the tailored suit she wore for her newspaper duties.

"Actually—it's what I can offer you." A conspiratorial smile tugged at her lips. "By the way, I love the sidewalk art."

She set her laptop bag on a chair.

All Olive could think about was the kids' chalk drawings. A ripple of unwarranted panic rose in her chest.

Kate's gaze softened, as if she could read Olive's thoughts.

"It's lovely. Lots of spring flowers. Definitely Annie approved."

Olive's heart rate eased. Would she ever stop worrying about being a nuisance?

"…and it's way too big for just me—so what do you think?"

Kate waited.

But Olive had drifted off again.

"I'm so sorry—what were you saying?"

Kate chuckled. "My journalist instincts say you were miles away." She winked. "And it's no secret a certain couple has been awfully chummy lately—"

Olive gasped. "Oh, mercy." Granddad's phrase, used often, slipped out before she could stop it. "Hank and I have a working relationship."

But for how long? Especially now that her doctor had told her to slow down.

"Uh-huh." Kate's knowing grin didn't help the swirl of questions Olive had been avoiding since their preserve outing.

"Anyway, I was saying the cottage I rent has two spare rooms." Kate adjusted the designer scarf slung over her shoulder.

"I'd be happy to sublet them to you and the kids—for a small fee."

That could solve their housing dilemma once their Hope House stay ended.

Her conversation with Eileen replayed—Olive admitting her uncertainty about staying in Sweetwater.

"And my landlord's fine with Roman, too."

Olive's heart swelled.

But before she could respond, Kate grabbed her laptop bag and slung the strap over her shoulder. "I'm off to an interview—but think about it."

"I will—thank you, Kate."

Wasn't it Hank who'd said it was okay to accept help?

At the door, Kate turned. "There's room for you and a bassinet in the second room, and the kids would have space of their own."

She smiled. "My brother left Josie's playset in the backyard after he sold the home he'd shared with his late wife."

An hour later, the conversation lingered in Olive's mind as she navigated Sweetwater's backstreets, heading toward the grocery store.

The kids chattered nonstop from the back seat.

The cottage idea held appeal. Especially with the baby gifts still stored at the firehouse.

She shook her head, remembering her reaction when she'd shown up to the Hot Mommas fundraiser and found out Hank had planned a surprise baby shower.

Another warning sign. She'd walked this road before.

The community's generosity reminded her of Donny's love early in their marriage.

Until he'd had enough.

She couldn't let the kids get hurt again. It was her job to protect them. To stay grounded in reality.

Because deep down, it always came back to her worthiness.

"Hey, Mom—I thought we were going to the farmers market?"

Simon leaned forward, peeking over the console.

Like her son, she preferred the buzz of the year-round market at Sweetwater Community College.

But the grocery store was faster.

"This'll be quicker—especially if you help me."

She parked, then grabbed her bag, the shopping list, and the funds from the committee.

As they crossed the lot, she paused to inhale the scent of orange blossoms—courtesy of the spring rains.

"Do we get a treat?"

Holly slipped her small hand into Olive's, flashing her gap-toothed grin.

Olive laughed, imagining Hank melting under that same smile.

"We live above a bakery with access to every sweet imaginable— and you *still* want a treat?" She rolled her eyes. "Come on, you two."

Simon grabbed her other hand, and they marched through the automatic doors.

Just inside, she handed baskets to each child and grabbed a cart.

"We need apples—lots of them."

She turned to Simon. "Can I trust you to watch your sister while I get the eggs?"

His little chest puffed up. "Yes, Mom."

She ruffled his unruly hair. "Good boy."

As she pushed the squeaky cart, her belly pressed against the handle.

"All in good time, little one," she whispered.

The store was quiet—it was a Thursday evening.

As she turned toward the dairy section, her thoughts drifted once more to the drive home from the preserve.

It was when she'd brought up Cartwright Realty with Hank.

She hadn't made headway at the shower.

And ever since, there hadn't been the right moment to broach the subject again.

Whether or not he took what she said with a grain of salt, she'd never forgive herself if she didn't give him a heads-up.

She stacked several cartons of eggs in her cart. Yet according to Annie—or had it been Lacey?—Slick had disappeared with a promise to follow up with Hank.

She'd already talked to Annie about keeping All American Auto from bulldozing Hank's ranch and taking over the small town.

But first—get her ducks in a row.

She giggled. Correction: chickens.

A few minutes later, she returned to the produce section to find Hank leaning over a wooden pallet—her kids close.

With their attention focused on a large yellowish-orange object balanced in Hank's broad hand, she approached unnoticed.

A label plastered on the side of the pallet identified the contents: dragon fruit.

Stepping behind a tall metal cart like the ones at the bakery, she took in the moment.

Hank passed the fruit to Simon, his voice low. "Remember that book about dragons you brought home from school?"

"I sure do!" Simon nodded eagerly.

"Feels like dragon skin—don't you think, son?"

Olive pressed her fingers to her lips to stifle a laugh. At the same time, her heart gave a small squeeze at Hank's ease with them.

Both kids' eyes bulged.

Holly bounced in place. "Can I touch it, too?"

Olive stepped out from behind the cart. "You've seen a lot of dragons, I take it?"

Bright pink patches bloomed across Hank's cheekbones.

She remembered a similar expression when he explained why Petey strutted his stuff.

Unfazed, Simon held out the dragon fruit with reverence. "It's got these spiny things and everything!"

She oohed and aahed before Hank plucked it from Simon's hand, returning it to the display. His attention shifted to her cart.

Right. Subject change.

She shrugged. "Oh, these? Egg hunt for the carnival—naturally."

She gestured at the bags of apples in their baskets. "Kids— load 'em up, please."

As they transferred the apples, her head felt…off.

A bead of sweat popped on her forehead.

She reached for the apple display to steady herself, and Hank caught her elbow.

"Olive—you don't look so good."

A mild cramp twisted in her belly. She squeezed her eyes shut. *It's too soon, Lord.*

When she opened them, three pairs of worried eyes stared back.

"I—I'm fine—"

A sharper pain doubled her over.

"That's it—I'm taking you to the ER."

She shook her head.

Her OB's instructions echoed in her mind—the lower back-ache she'd brushed off, the lightheadedness she'd ignored.

"Let me check if my OB is on call—please."

An ER visit would wipe out her funds.

But Hank's furrowed brow and grim set mouth left no room for argument.

"Mommy?"

Holly's small hand patted her back, fear quivering in that one word.

As another cramp built, a headache pulsed behind Olive's eyes.

Kate appeared out of nowhere, taking in the scene with a quick scan.

Hank filled her in, and Jack's sister nodded, promising to stay with the kids.

Olive was fairly certain Hank had broken a few traffic laws before they skidded into the ER lot.

Once her OB met them at the entrance, the worst had passed.

Still, the doctor led Olive to a cubby and drew the curtain.

God, please let my baby be okay.

Not long after, Olive stood at the front desk, settling the bill.

So much for those hand-stitched boots.

Dehydration, she sighed.

How could I be so careless?

"You're sure the baby is healthy?"

Hank glanced at her sideways from the driver's seat, concern still etched into his features.

Her cheeks burned.

Or maybe it was just the man beside her causing the lingering flush.

Shadows stretched across the dashboard as the sun dipped behind the mountains. She offered a tired smile.

"But I heard something about bed rest—"

Her OB had mentioned that. She wrinkled her nose and mumbled something.

There was no way she was missing the carnival.

Still, she'd agreed to stay off her feet at work.

As Hank turned onto Main Street, a flash of blue in a shop window caught her eye.

"Stop here—please!"

He hit the brakes in front of Twice-Loved Treasures.

The driver behind them leaned on their horn. Hank waved them past.

A pair of cowgirl boots with turquoise stitching gleamed in the display. Trinkets and treasures sparkled from the velvet throws.

Hank growled low beside her. The grizzly bear she'd come to know and—

She swallowed hard.

Nope. Not going there. Her dehydration was clearly still messing with her.

He'd swung back to the market to hitch up her SUV and now pulled to the curb, staying put when she asked.

By the time she stepped out of the shop, a bag in hand, only a few minutes had passed.

"I hope you're happy," Hank grumbled, pulling behind the bakery.

"Thank you," she murmured, a soft smile teasing her lips.

Mr. Timmons had sold her the boots at a fraction of what she'd seen in the boutique.

She unbuckled and waited for Hank to round the vehicle.

When his fingers brushed hers, her stomach fluttered—and this time it wasn't from a cramp.

She couldn't ignore the butterflies. Or deny the truth creeping in at the edges.

She might have fallen for Hank.

Which left her suspended somewhere between fear—and the peace that passes all understanding.

* * *

Hank swiped his mouth with the back of his hand. If he had to drink one more ounce of the inn's sweet water—

The councilman's wife was gonna get an earful.

And not because she'd donated the beverages to the carnival.

No—from his racing heart to his trouble breathing around a certain expectant mother, he suspected he was already a goner.

A casualty of the town legend. Despite his attempts to fight it.

Olive had stuck with some fruity concoction at the shower— an avoidance of all things myth-related.

Which wouldn't have been a big deal, except he'd come to realize she and her kids were what had been missing from his life.

His heart was no longer bound by grief. And he had no clue what to do about it.

He chucked the bottle into a nearby recycling bin in the church parking lot.

It had just been him and a few volunteers at dawn.

Now, the grounds teemed with adults and kids swarming the booths.

Persh joined him and clapped him on the back.

"So where's your date?" His eyes scanned the crowd.

Hank choked back a cough, his gaze landing on the object of his thoughts.

She was perched on a stool a couple of booths over.

Deep in concentration, she applied face paint to the next child in a long line waiting for their turn.

Heat crept up his neck. "Who said Olive and I are on a date?"

Persh's hearty guffaw confirmed Hank's blunder.

"Right..." The councilman winked, then pointed to the booth next door. A barrel of water reflected the midmorning sun, shiny red apples bobbing on the surface.

Holly and Simon waved from their places in line.

"Looks like the chief needs an extra hand—" Persh swiped a palm across his goatee "—but if you need any pointers..." He waggled his eyebrows in Olive's direction.

Before Hank could respond, Persh walked off—his laughter trailing behind.

Leaving Hank downright grumpy.

Since picking up the Harts and arriving earlier this morning, he and Olive had been swept up in the carnival flurry—with no time to themselves.

They'd been tied up at their respective booths, supervising Holly and Simon, or taking turns with Roman.

But that was about to change.

He hadn't spent the early morning hours throwing on a half dozen shirts—or fiddling with one of the constable's bolo ties until his patience frayed like the leather tips—for nothing.

Which was how he'd clipped his scruff so close it barely reached a few inches from his chin.

Out of habit, his fingers went to it.

He grimaced when they brushed the short hairs, unable to give them a good tug.

It had been worth it just to see Olive's shy smile when he helped her into the truck.

"Oh, my—don't you clean up."

And to hear the approval tucked between the lines.

It had taken everything in him not to stare at the hand-stitched boots. Her long legs peeking out from the floral knit maternity dress. Feminine curves.

He scrubbed at the prickles on his neck and straightened his back.

Marched toward the face-painting station.

Off to the side, Holly's squeal squeezed his heart.

A red flag.

It wasn't just his feelings—or Olive's—on the line.

Not when news traveled like wildfire in these parts.

"Hey, you." A caramel lock fell across Olive's cheek as she lifted her head.

His fingers twitched, almost reaching to tuck it behind an ear.

"No butting in," she added, golden eyes twinkling.

He released a nervous chuckle.

Stationed beside her chair, Roman gave him a long, probing look.

Every line he'd rehearsed vanished.

To anyone else, he'd blame the blank-out on the sticky-sweet scent of cotton candy carried on the breeze. Or the canned carnival music playing on loop from the speakers.

Roman let out a sharp bark, and Hank snapped out of it.

Olive had turned back to the orange and blue butterfly she painted with careful strokes on a little girl's cheek.

He cleared his throat, and the Lab untangled himself, loping over to Hank and pressing his big head against his leg.

Hank dropped a hand to Roman's head—just in time to catch Olive stretching, pressing her knuckles against her lower back.

Then flash him a smile that rivaled any sunrise.

Get a grip, Big Country.

"Do you get—" His voice cracked. He coughed into the sleeve of the polo shirt he'd paired with khakis. "A break soon?"

She giggled.

An endearing sound that nearly made up for his subpar social skills.

"You must've heard my stomach growling."

Mrs. Greer appeared from the sidelines. "Go have fun now, honey."

Olive grinned and slid off the chair. "I guess she told me."

Then—without missing a beat—the next volunteer claimed her seat, and her fingers were threaded through his.

Just like at the preserve.

All his senses zeroed in on her small hand folded into his.

He hadn't been exaggerating when he'd said he was rusty at this dating thing.

It had been Louie's spitball that kept him from crossing the line. Then, Simon's innocent question on the drive home.

How did you explain something you didn't fully understand yourself?

What he *did* understand: loss. Betrayal.

And Olive did, too.

His business had been the constant. The purpose that kept him afloat all these years.

She tugged him to the food and beverage station.

No plans had ever made room for family. For love.

"These smell so good," she said, pulling him from his distracted thoughts.

The yeasty aroma of Annie's sourdough pretzels made his mouth water.

She finished hers and smacked her lips. "That was delicious—thank you."

He glanced at his empty wrapper and chuckled. "I guess I must've thought so, too."

It'd be easier to focus on work if she weren't so adorable. If she hadn't taken his hand again.

They spent the next hour or so wandering from booth to booth—from the cupcake "waddle," aptly named by Annie with a teasing grin, to the egg hunt Simon and Holly joined alongside dozens of other kids, to the beanbag toss popular with guests of all ages.

Don't let me lose sight of what's important, Lord.

The silent prayer warred with goals he'd had well before the Harts came to town.

Olive had long since fulfilled their working arrangement.

He tried convincing himself he was just doing her a favor. Not for self-serving reasons.

Which fooled no one.

Especially not Gordie, judging by the looks he shot Hank whenever Olive's name came up.

"Where to next?"

Olive's voice jolted him back to the present.

He was about to answer when Holly and Simon skipped over, baskets looped over their skinny arms, hard-boiled eggs nestled inside.

She dropped his hand.

The sudden chill that remained said more than words.

"Can we color these now?" Holly's wide eyes sparkled with excitement.

Noticing the slight sag in Olive's shoulders, he hoisted both kids into his arms.

"You go rest your feet, and we'll meet you at the photo booth in thirty minutes."

She gave him a tired but grateful smile.

For the next half hour, he helped Holly and Simon decorate eggs with organic dyes from the bakery.

The longest thirty minutes he could remember—though in reality, any day she spent holed up at the computer instead of the shop felt even longer. Still, it was for her own good.

While they waited for Olive at the photo booth, the kids posed with Polly—a rescue parrot with a long, sweeping tail.

Everyone wanted a picture with the bird dressed in iridescent green, yellow, red, and blue.

A tap on his shoulder sent his heart into a sprint.

But when he turned, it wasn't Olive. It was the constable.

"Got a second?" Jack pushed the brim of his Stetson higher.

"Yeah—what's up?"

His attention drifted toward Olive as she approached, one hand resting on her belly.

"Heard you're selling the ranch to Cartwright…"

Jack rocked back on his worn cowboy boots. The badge pinned to his collar caught a glint of sun.

Hank snorted. "Anyone at all *not* privy to my business?"

The constable chuckled. "Not likely. But I did ask my PI buddy Toby to look into this realty guy."

His ice-blue stare hit Hank dead center. Left him uneasy.

It was the same topic Olive had tried to bring up. One he'd shut down every time.

"You know they're a front for All American Auto."

Hank's thoughts turned to mud.

The implications struck hard.

A national chain—known for crushing mom-and-pop shops.

Hadn't the last incident been in Snowpeak? Olive's hometown?

He swallowed the lump rising in his throat.

Jack elbowed his side as the Harts got closer. "Olive is a special lady—isn't she?"

"Huh?" Hank jerked his head up—met her sparkling eyes.

"Squawk! Olive's a special lady—squawk!"

The kids burst out laughing at Polly's surprise shout.

Liquid heat surged through his veins when Olive's lips curved into a smile.

"Just make sure you know what you're doing," Jack said.

Then he slipped away to help a handler with the parrot, leaving Hank to stew in his thoughts as the Harts joined him.

What *was* he doing?

With Cartwright, sure.

But mostly—with her. Thinking about a future he hadn't planned on.

"Mr. Big—let's get a picture with Polly!"

Which was how he ended up at the front of the line. The bright white light of the flash—capturing his emotions in a photo that the kids squealed over.

But it was the flush on Olive's cheeks he didn't dare read into.

It dogged his heels all the way to the apartment. On the drive over, Olive had tried—again—to tell him about Cartwright Realty, her voice carrying urgency. He only half-registered the snippets as his mind churned through the garage and the kids. But he already knew the truth, didn't he? That the company was in direct cahoots with All American.

Olive fumbled with her key in the lock, Roman at her feet. The kids had gone to the Wellses' for a sleepover.

At the sound of the latch, understanding cracked open the missing link in his life.

Family.

She pushed open the door a crack and turned her head, unaware that a single look had his pulse spiking.

"I'm sorry you had to cut out early on my account."

He shrugged and shoved his hands in his pockets. "Should be headin' back to the garage—"

He could've mentioned the PI's findings. But a split second later, she faced him, close enough that he could see the gold flecks in her eyes through dark lashes.

"Thank you for a lovely day, Hank."

She stretched up on booted toes. Bridged the half foot between them.

Pressed soft lips to his. A featherlight kiss.

One he'd replay until he could convince himself it hadn't been imagined.

But Roman's expression—when the big lug followed Olive inside and the door closed softly behind them—was all the proof he needed.

As if Hank had somehow earned his way out of the doghouse.

With a new lightness in his step, he took the stairs two at a time.

Until truth hit him like a freight train.

Even the clink of silverware and muted laughter on the café patio couldn't drown out the warning bells.

Falling for Olive and her kids didn't fit into his well-ordered life.

But her kiss had changed everything.

Okay, Lord—I surrender my plans for Yours.

He snorted. Hadn't his friends been telling him the same thing from the start?

Back at the garage, he pulled on his coveralls—his prayer on repeat.

Then shot off a text to his contact at Cartwright.

One decision down. Two remaining.

If Olive and her kids planned to stay in Sweetwater long enough for him to fix his heart.

And if he could keep the garage afloat without the sale.

After finishing Miss Marie's complimentary oil change, he pulled out his phone.

A text from Cartwright Realty blinked on the screen.

A confirmation that his earlier message turning down the offer had been received.

He tapped the thread—and his jaw dropped.

Just saw your msg, came after the deadline.
No reply = acceptance. Cartwright's got your holdings locked.
Paperwork to follow. If you have ques—

The rest swam before his eyes.

God, what have I done?

He dropped to his knees in the middle of his shop.

Except for the formalities—the actual exchange of money— silence had sealed it. He'd as good as sold out. *Literally.*

His stomach churned.

So much for surrendering my plans for Yours.

Even if he could come up with the funds to expand the garage, they couldn't compete with the national chain.

Worse?

He had nothing to offer Olive or her kids. Except maybe himself.

A midlife, washed-up mechanic. A failing business.

The budget-hotel-sized room in the back of the garage.

And no idea how long even that would be in the picture.

Chapter Ten

Olive logged out of the garage's software program—a skill that had become second nature.

She grabbed a bottle of the sweet water Annie kept stocked in her apartment—and guzzled it.

Against her better judgment, she'd given in to its flavor. Maybe even the promise of true love.

Once she finally accepted her growing feelings for Hank.

Now, she followed Angel—their newly hired apprentice— into the first bay.

The lingering scents hit her first—nostalgia, then a niggle of guilt. She'd agreed to stay out of the shop after the last scare.

But Angel had only asked her to take a quick look at his work.

Gordie and Hank were tied up in a meeting with Jack at the municipal building. She'd had to pry a little. Eventually, Hank mumbled something about seeking legal counsel.

At the back of the garage, she snagged a small tray of tools and followed Angel to a vehicle suspended on a lift.

She balanced the tray on her belly and went to work confirming he'd disconnected the proper wires, loosened the belts, and removed the mounting bolts.

Straightening, she wiped her palms on her coveralls and smiled.

"When Gordie returns, you're all set to replace the alternator."

Angel beamed.

"Thanks, Ms. Olive."

"Still check with one of the guys since I'm 'banned' from the shop." She winked, fingers forming air quotes.

But her smile didn't quite reach her eyes.

Ever since the spring carnival, Hank had been distant, distracted at best.

She could at least blame her own daydreaming on the spontaneous kiss she'd planted on his mouth.

Even now, the memory made her cheeks warm and her heart skip a beat.

She hadn't stuck around to gauge his reaction. And he never brought it up.

If anything, he'd grown grumpier—probably because of what she'd said about Cartwright, even though he seemed a million miles away—doing nothing but fuel her insecurities.

"You'd better get back out there," Angel said.

Too late.

The door flung open with a bang, slapping hard against the wall.

"What's going on in here?" Hank's voice held an edge of restrained anger.

At the sound of it, her baby kicked, and the tray on her belly wobbled.

Three pairs of eyes watched as it clattered to the cement floor.

"Wicked!" Angel breathed, eyes wide.

She giggled nervously, lifting her hands. "I just finished checking our apprentice's work, boss."

Hank's jaw clenched, and he tugged on the collar of his plaid button-down.

Tucked into a pair of Wranglers for his morning appointment, he looked more like the lumberjack Simon had first imagined.

A tall, ginger, ruggedly handsome lumberjack.

She pressed her lips together to keep from smiling.

"At your computer now—please."

Uh-oh.

The man was *not* amused.

He didn't wait for a reply—just stormed off the floor.

The door rattled shut, and she crouched to gather the scattered tools. But before her fingers found the wrench, a sharp pain sliced through her core.

Her knees buckled. And she went down. Hard.

"Ms. Olive! Big Country!" Angel rushed to her side, hovering.

She tried to offer a reassuring word, but all she could do was breathe.

The door creaked again. Boots thundered across the floor.

"What happened?" Panic warred with gruffness in Hank's voice.

Worn work boots swam in her vision.

"She just fell, sir—I don't…"

Hank dropped beside her, sliding a hand beneath her arms.

His voice softened to a near whisper. "Okay if I help you up?"

She nodded quickly, swallowing against a surge of nausea.

In one swift motion, he lifted her into his arms like she weighed nothing.

His coarse beard brushed her cheek. She shivered.

"Are you cold? Dehydrated?"

She shook her head, swallowing again as bile burned her throat.

Since her scare at the market, she'd tried to stay hydrated.

To stay off her feet more.

But with two kids—and the baby keeping her up nights—that was easier said than done.

Another cramp gripped her abdomen and crawled down her back.

She knew this feeling. It wasn't dehydration.

Oh, Lord, I'm not due for three weeks.

But just because Holly and Simon had arrived late didn't mean Baby Hart was on the same schedule.

She squeezed her eyes shut and rode out the contraction.

Please keep my baby safe.

The distant whine of sirens grew louder.

She opened her eyes, focusing on the solid strength of Hank's arms until the pain passed.

Memories and questions swirled in her mind.

Even when he kept his distance, she'd seen how he looked at her.

Like maybe…maybe he *wanted* something more.

At first, that terrified her. The ink on her divorce papers had barely dried the day she fled Snowpeak.

But now, as his light blue eyes met hers, emotion surged in their depths.

Weighty.

Grief and bone-deep fear etched hard lines into his face.

It gutted her. She had to look away.

Pulling double duty as both firefighter and paramedic, Chad Harrington hustled through the door. Without ceremony, she was transferred to a gurney.

The apology on her lips dissolved beneath the next contraction.

"Explain to me again why we couldn't move into Kate's cottage?"

From her nest of pillows on Hank's sofa, Olive swept her eyes over the lived-in space.

Outside, the kids played within clear view, tossing a rubber ball to each other across the field.

Their laughter drifted in with the breeze, mingling with Roman's happy barks.

Next to her on the scuffed coffee table, a serving platter held a pitcher of ice-cold sweet water—Lacey's doing.

It had been a few days since the false labor scare. A few days of settling back into Hank's home—and into something that felt dangerously close to hope.

A crease settled between Hank's eyes.

"Termites."

Olive groaned.

The kids loved the change in scenery. But mandatory bed rest hadn't been part of her plan. Funds were tight.

She'd been counting on a few more weeks of income from helping Annie with event planning.

Even though she'd already paid off her car repairs through the garage, at least Hank still insisted on paying her.

And the Lord had carried them this far.

"Can I get you anything before I leave?"

She scanned the stack of puzzle books and magazines he'd picked up for her and shook her head.

All the trouble she'd put him through. Again.

"Miss Marie should be here any minute."

She formed a pout. "I don't need a babysitter, you know."

His smile didn't reach his eyes. "It's her cleaning day."

"Uh-huh." She gave him a look. "I wasn't born yesterday."

She gave a soft huff. Then turned her head away, absently watching Roman leap for the ball.

One good thing about bed rest? More time to dream.

Her thoughts shifted to her idea for turning Hank's barn into an income-producing venue.

Her spirits lifted—just a smidge.

"Any interest yet in refurbishing the old barn?"

Facing him, she pulled a tasseled pillow to her chest.

"It just needs a new roof, a few cedar boards swapped out, a fresh coat of paint, and—"

"I appreciate your enthusiasm, Olive—but it's not happening."

His beard swallowed the corners of his mouth as he clamped his jaw shut and shook his head.

"Yes, it'll take work, Hank—but I heard how everyone helped renovate the preserve's live-in quarters…and Annie's café…"

Why did this matter so much to her?

Approval. A purpose. Something more than just her roles as a mother or mechanic.

Hank's shoulders dipped. Regret clouded his gaze.

"That meeting this week—the one with the constable?"

Had it really only been seventy-two hours since she'd gone into preterm labor?

Her OB had confirmed it once she'd arrived at the hospital—by fire engine, no less.

Simon was still disappointed he'd missed the *adventure*. She snorted softly at the memory.

"—so unless Jack finds a loophole in Cartwright's paperwork, the ranch is as good as sold."

What?

Didn't Annie mention something similar back when Josh was awarded custody of his foster brother's son?

Some legal glitch that required him to marry—or risk losing Finn. In the end, it had all worked out.

She adjusted a pillow behind her and squared her shoulders.

If there's a will, there's a way.

Her Granddad's words. They'd comforted her after Donny's desertion…after his passing…and again when the Lord led her to Hope House. Eventually, to Sweetwater.

"But when I get back to the garage—"

Hank sliced a hand through the air. "You're not coming back."

"Excuse me?"

The sliding door cracked open. Simon's head poked in.

"Mom—can we have a sleepover with Josie and Anthony?"

Holly pressed up behind him on the cement pad, their faces flushed with exertion.

Roman bounded across the threshold, lunging straight for Hank.

Traitor.

A low-grade pressure built up at her temples. "This isn't our home, kids."

Her eyes landed on the dog—flat on his back, blissfully enjoying Hank's scratches behind his ears.

"And please take Roman back outside while I finish my talk with—Mr. Hank."

Both kids grumbled.

"You heard your mother." Hank shooed Roman out the door and closed it.

Olive's gaze followed her children, a small swell of relief settling in her chest.

It had been a long time since she'd had backup.

But how long could she manage on bed rest?

Be careful for nothing.

Her Granddad's wisdom poked a hole in the anxiety bubbling to the surface.

She turned back to Hank, whose silence spoke louder than the kids' shouts and laughter.

His jaw relaxed.

Her pulse quickened.

Had her kiss meant anything to him?

He swiped a hand through his short-cropped hair and released a tired breath.

"As long as you're under my roof—it's your home, too."

His words landed close. The stuff of her daydreams, now tangled with the fear of overstaying their welcome.

She turned her head, her gaze sweeping over the butter-hued field stretching clear to the mountains.

But in every thing by prayer and supplication with thanksgiving...

She peeked at him over her shoulder. "But the garage is off-limits." It wasn't a question.

He gave a slow, gentle nod.

"Your employment there…paused for now."

Her heart lurched. His gaze drifted outdoors.

How could he do this to her after everything?

She cleared her throat. "What about the internship?"

Slowly, he met her eyes—his filled with regret. Hopes deferred. Defeat.

The same emotions she'd battled from her perch on the sofa, somehow tangled up with All American Auto—maybe even the beginning of the end for Hank & Gordie's.

His Adam's apple dipped before he spoke again.

"The shop can't handle the risk—not with your family in the picture."

Family.

His voice cracked on the word—her chest squeezed.

A palpable awareness pulsed between them.

Just then, a rat-a-tat-tat on the service door echoed through the breezeway.

"It's just me!"

Miss Marie stepped in from the garage carrying a dish topped with aluminum foil.

The door closed behind her as she set the casserole on the washing machine and slipped out of her shoes.

Hank turned back to Olive. "The shop can't afford the liability."

Olive's lips parted on a sharp gasp—her breath hitching.

He couldn't have spelled out his true feelings any clearer.

Liability equals burden.

Lowering her voice, she pushed past his rugged looks and the teddy bear heart beneath the surface.

"You don't have to worry—" she hiccupped, blinking back tears. "I'll be out of your hair as soon as Kate's cottage is habitable."

Hank flinched.

"For good."

His jaw hardened. His eyes darkened with pain. Maybe even longing.

Just then, Miss Marie stepped into the kitchen, her eyes snapping toward the living area.

She must've felt the tension—thick enough to cut with a butter knife.

Olive caught the way Hank curled his fingers into fists.

A frisson of guilt pierced her chest.

And then he pivoted on his heel and brushed past the older woman.

A loud crack. Glass shattering.

Olive swung her gaze toward the picture window.

She was sure the children's ball had broken the glass.

But the sudden ache behind her rib cage said otherwise.

It was her heart that had shattered.

The final passage of Philippians 4:6 washed over her.

Amid dreams of love and a tug-of-war between fear and peace, she'd forgotten the key directive: to bring her requests before God.

Miss Marie's questioning gaze pierced the moment.

But first, Olive bowed her head.

And cried out from a bruised and willing heart.

Hank grasped the grab handle and swung into the driver's seat. He pulled the door closed. Swiped at his beard.

"What have I done, God?"

He pinched his eyes shut and replayed the words he'd wielded. A single sentence that had sabotaged whatever had been developing between them.

The one woman who'd ever truly understood him.

Honestly? He'd known what he was doing from the get-go. It was what he always did. And he'd gotten the reaction he expected.

Never mind that he'd started to believe—maybe, just maybe—he could offer the Harts the home they deserved.

Love.

Thanks to the kiss that had rocked his world and hinted at what might be possible.

But instead, it only proved his brokenness.

He dropped his head to the steering wheel and groaned.

"Mr. Big!"

Hank lifted his head as if it weighed a ton. Peeled open his eyes.

Simon's innocent face appeared at his window, Holly and Roman by his side.

He unlatched the door, and they squeezed closer.

"Mom is sleeping, and Miss Marie is cleaning—can we come with you?"

Holly flashed her gap-toothed smile. "Please?"

Five seconds. That's how long it took to decide.

He reached behind him and pushed open the back door. "Climb aboard."

"Yay!"

Roman woofed as they crawled onto the seats.

Hank fired off a quick text to Gordie at the garage, who was with Angel and another mentee from The Lodge.

A thumbs-up came fast.

He sent another message to Miss Marie, stuffing his regrets about Olive—and the Cartwright mess that still sat wrong with him—into the far corner of his mind, for now.

He clapped his hands. "All buckled?"

The kids nodded.

He cranked the engine. "All right, where to, guys?"

"Can we go fishin' again?"

Simon's grin was all eagerness, like Hank's had been as a kid with his dad.

He hesitated. How would Olive feel about an impromptu lake trip?

"Tell you what—once your momma's back on her feet, we'll plan something special."

But then what? He snapped his fingers.

"Sit tight—you're in for a fun time."

He steered them toward Main Street, where banners fluttered from the lampposts. The weekly arts and crafts festival in Town Square was back.

"Will there be face painting, too?" Holly piped up.

He caught her reflection in the mirror—golden-brown pigtails bouncing, adorable grin wide. She looked so much like a younger Josie, it caused his heart to squeeze. Jack had learned to braid like a pro after losing his wife.

"How about we find out?"

They rolled along, orange blossoms scenting the breeze through the open windows—fresh, sweet. Like Olive. All sunshine and warmth.

His jaw flexed. Maybe not now.

"Wow!" the kids shouted.

He parked a few blocks down, and they crossed the busy intersection.

Town Square overflowed with people and color. The spring carnival couldn't hold a candle to this.

Booths lined the block—artists painting at easels, others selling candles, salsa, and beaded jewelry.

But not Annie's bakery this weekend.

The kids spotted the gazebo and took off running.

A cowboy perched on the steps strummed a guitar, his hat on the ground full of bills and coins.

Hank trailed after them, slowing as he reached the constable on duty.

Jack leaned against his police cruiser, parked sideways to block off Main Street. "Good to see you again," he said, pumping Hank's hand.

He tugged off his Stetson, slapped it against his thigh, then raked a hand through short curls.

Hank's gaze drifted to the kids and Roman, stationed near the singing cowboy. He grunted in agreement. Their last meeting about Cartwright hadn't exactly been all hearts and flowers.

"Let me guess—Ms. Hart's idea?" Jack turned back with a smirk.

Shaking his head, Hank shoved his hands in his pockets. "Only because she's on bed rest and—"

Jack lifted a hand. "Say no more. You feel responsible." He slid the hat back on.

Why wouldn't he? The scare at the market had rattled him more than he cared to admit.

Since then, he'd done everything he could to make it right. Kept her off her feet at the shop. Arranged help. Occupied the kids. And then she'd gone into early labor on his watch.

Still, the what-ifs taunted him. What if he'd been on a tow that morning…?

He glanced toward the gazebo again.

"I feel responsible for finding a way out of the mess with Cartwright," he muttered.

Jack hooked his thumb in his belt loop and rocked back on his boots.

"Funny you say that. I've got good news, buddy."

Hank's chest eased. Hope flickered.

"I'm all ears."

Jack grinned. "Not since your hair grew out and covered your bald head."

Hank rolled his eyes. "Hilarious. Go on."

Jack's attention shifted to a group of teens gathered near the old Town Square building.

"Looks like we've got our guy—on a technicality." He turned back. "Just confirming with my PI friend."

Loud voices interrupted them. A few teens scrambled onto the statue of Lacey's ancestor, Sweetwater's founder. Others zipped down the steps on skateboards.

"I'd better get over there before someone breaks a neck." Jack clapped him on the shoulder and moved off the curb.

A few yards away, under a perfect blue sky, Simon and Holly watched a father and son fly a kite.

He swallowed hard.

If Jack was right, he might not lose the ranch.

His gut twisted. But what did it matter now?

He'd called Olive a liability. Said the one thing she'd feared most.

And maybe sealed his fate. At least where she was concerned.

He groaned. Hadn't he already learned that his overprotectiveness drove people away?

"Big Country!"

A female voice interrupted his pity party. He lifted his head.

Annie, her face glowing, carried an insulated bag stamped with the bakery's bright pink logo.

"Hey, Annie—thought you'd have a booth today."

She brushed a wisp of hair off her forehead. "Oh, a couple of boys from The Lodge are handing out coupons." She winked. "For free lemon bars at the shop."

Now *that* was speaking his language.

Her gray-blue eyes sparkled. "So, how's our patient doing?"

"Miss Marie's at the ranch—cleaning."

Annie chuckled. "Smart move." She pointed toward the municipal offices. "I've got to drop this off—but make time to talk soon—Olive's got ideas for renovating your old barn."

"Oh, Annie." He coughed into his sleeve. "No offense, but—"

She gave his forearm a quick squeeze. "It would really help me out, Hank." A sigh slipped from her lips. "I've had so many catering requests, the café's bursting at the seams."

He did the math. If Jack was right—and that was still a big "if"—the money he had wouldn't stretch past a lick of paint.

Annie nodded, eyes full of understanding, as if she'd read his mind.

"Persh already promised to loan muscle from The Lodge, and—"

He drew in a deep breath. "Unless Jack confirms I'm in the clear with Cartwright and All American Auto…"

Annie's lips flattened. "Hmm. Okay." She pushed her frames up, considering the next steps. "While we wait for our legal extraordinaire to come through—" a grin broke across her face "—as you know, I happen to throw a mean fundraiser!"

He laughed. "I can vouch for that."

Over Labor Day weekend, she'd organized a combo fundraiser and grand opening of Annie's Café.

The proceeds had kept Hope House running, the nonprofit that had placed her baby with a forever family when she'd been a pregnant teen.

A reminder of what his own life lacked. A lump rose in his throat.

"—and remember when the town council almost closed the preserve?"

Memories surfaced of the town rallying.

He appreciated her enthusiasm. But it all hinged on Jack's findings.

"I've got to run, but look…" Her gaze met his. "When Josh was injured on duty, you helped make my café a reality." She paused. "When will you let others step in for a change?"

Hadn't he told Olive the same thing?

If Jack was right—

He should be ready. Ready to expand. To set Gordie up for retirement.

He pictured the Harts—all they represented.

Lord, am I a fool to hope for…

He shrugged and lifted one corner of his mouth. "What did you have in mind?"

Her eyes beamed. She winked. "Let me take care of that."

As she stepped away, he called, "What can I do?"

Before she disappeared into the stream of pedestrians, she turned back and mouthed a single word: "Pray."

Just then, Olive's trio darted toward him, gasping for breath as they grabbed his hands.

He had just enough time to whisper a prayer.

Okay, God. Your will, not mine.

During the following two hours, they visited each booth at least once.

By the time the sun dipped toward the horizon—tummies and pockets full—they were headed home along the two-lane highway.

The kids drifted off. His thoughts wandered…

To the velvet brush of Olive's lips on his cheek.

To the betrayal in her eyes.

He vaguely registered passing Sweetwater Lake.

"Mr. Big!"

He felt the tug on his shirtsleeve—heard the scream. And locked on to two scared eyes staring down his fifteen-ton truck.

He cranked the wheel.

Protect us, Lord.

Later, he'd replay the seconds.

The jolt over the embankment. Tires lifting. Branches screeching. His teeth rattling as the truck lurched down the rocky slope.

A hard stop. The seat belt caught.

Oomph.

Not more than a few yards ahead, low branches scraped his hood.

Holly's soft cry. Simon's steady reassurances.

Heart pounding, Hank twisted to face them. "You guys okay?" His voice was shaky.

Wide eyes nodded back.

Thank You, God.

The hook and ladder appeared seemingly out of nowhere.

When Josh and the paramedic agreed that the kids should be checked at Sweetwater General, it had turned into an adventure for them. For him? His boots wore a path in the waiting room carpet.

"The chief gave me the skinny." Jack slipped beside him, matching his pace. "Kids are okay."

Relief washed over Hank. He nodded.

"You've got your truck to deal with. I can get 'em back to the ranch."

Hank felt the weight of Jack's stare. Could he face Olive after this?

He swallowed hard and scrubbed at his beard.

"Much obliged."

Jack squeezed his shoulder, stopping him. "Can I speak as your friend?"

Hank grimaced. "Can I stop you?"

Jack chuckled. "Now who's hilarious?" His tone sobered. Eyes sharp.

Maybe too sharp.

"When Em got hurt, and Josie sprained her wrist…"

Jack looked off, lost in memory.

"Pastor Mark told me something I'll never forget. I'd been trying to play God—under the guise of serving and protecting."

"But I'm not—"

Jack shook his head. "Maybe not. But while you're busy fixing everyone else, you've been neglecting yourself."

He tilted the brim of his Stetson.

"What if you let God step in? Let Him love you into healing?"

Without another word, Jack walked toward the information desk.

Hank stepped through the automatic doors. The sun had dipped below the horizon.

While he waited for Gordie, Jack's words buzzed in his ears. Memories swarmed.

Snow and sleet. A deserted stretch of highway. Rosie's crash.

The image morphed—he remembered the buck's six-foot rack cutting across his vision that afternoon.

Then another winter storm, his dad coaching him through slippery roads.

"Just remember, son—every vehicle is equal on ice."

His dad's tone had been commanding.

Clarity slammed into him. He jolted to a stop.

Yes—Rosie had defied him. But the truth?

There'd always been one unpredictable loose thread in the tapestry of that day.

The buck. No one could've predicted it.

On a road they'd driven a hundred times.

I've blamed myself all these years, Lord.

Channeled the guilt into "fixing."

Had Jack been right? Had the Lord placed the Harts in his life to guide him toward healing?

He'd called her a liability. Jeopardized the kids' safety.

Could she forgive him?

He took a breath. Made up his mind.

Ranch or no ranch—

He had a business to run. Dreams to pursue. And this time?

The Harts were part of those dreams.

He only hoped Olive felt the same.

Chapter Eleven

She jerked awake. Shapeless dreams scattered into the corners.

Olive peeled her eyes open. Something was wrong.

Where am I?

Her gaze locked onto Miss Marie, legs tucked under her on the easy chair.

Memories drifted through the haze of Hank reading to Simon and Holly in that same chair, the kids pressed close.

Their last conversation slammed into her. The images dissolved, and her heart squeezed.

Miss Marie marked her place in the Bible open on her lap. Peeked up.

"You're still here." Olive cleared her throat.

The older woman smiled gently and nodded. She set the Bible on the coffee table beside the untouched magazines, then poured a glass of tepid sweet water and handed it to Olive.

Shadows stretched across the room, confirming her suspicions. No way had Miss Marie spent the entire afternoon cleaning.

To anyone else, the gesture looked sincere. Sweet. If it weren't for Hank's betrayal.

"Liability," he'd said.

Olive blinked. Turned her head. Scanned the empty field.

The silence must've roused her. A flash of panic zinged through her chest.

She met Miss Marie's steady gaze. "Where are my kids?"

The woman eased out of the chair and tucked a crocheted afghan around Olive's shoulders.

"Holly and Simon are just fine, dear."

The soft yarn brushed her neck—a shower gift from Emerson that matched another for Baby Hart.

Miss Marie's soothing voice loosened the knot in Olive's chest.

"The constable should be dropping them off any minute." Her hazel eyes twinkled with understanding.

"Why are they with Jack?"

"They had themselves a bit of an adventure—"

Olive listened as Miss Marie recounted the hours since she'd fallen asleep.

Her heart pounded hard, momma bear instincts pulsing as she waited to confirm her kids were safe.

By the time she returned from the restroom, she'd worked herself into a near panic.

A large buck, the tow truck plunging off the road.

But the driver and passengers were unharmed.

Thank You, sweet Jesus.

That didn't explain how the kids had ended up in Hank's care.

Despite his hurtful words, she bowed her head. Prayed like her life depended on it.

Offered gratitude for God's faithfulness in the darkest moments.

Petitioned for strength to forgive—

Hank. Her mom. The man who walked out before she was born. The kids' dad.

Her twin sister for not surviving.

"Amen."

Barking and animated chatter drifted from the breezeway. Music to her ears. Her eyes snapped open.

"Sounds like your bear cubs are home." Miss Marie patted Olive's hand and turned toward the entryway.

Home.

A dream that had crashed and burned.

"Mommy, Mommy!"

Holly and Simon dove straight for the sofa. Roman trailed behind—tongue lolling, tail wagging.

Holly clamped her arms around Olive's baby bump, pressed her cheek close, then dropped to her knees.

Her world righted.

Olive skimmed her fingers over the Labrador's boxy head.

"Mom, you should have seen it!" Simon paused, catching his breath. "That buck was *'gantic* and we went *flyin'* in the air, and then the fire truck came and—"

She winced at the picture her son painted. Her gaze lifted. Landed on the constable, who leaned against the doorjamb.

"Thank you," she mouthed.

"Ma'am." He wiped his boots on the entry rug and removed his Stetson before entering the living area.

"Mr. Jack brought us home in his police cruiser!"

A dark lock fell across Simon's forehead. She brushed it out of his eyes.

Her heart seized at the thought of a very different ending to the story.

"Kids, you must be starving after all your excitement today."

Bless Miss Marie's heart. She ushered the children toward the dining area—leaving Olive and the constable alone.

Jack cleared his throat. "Hank couldn't feel worse about what happened—would've driven them back himself, but…"

She chewed her bottom lip. The man must be consumed with guilt.

"Ironically, he had to get a tow out of the ravine." Jack's gaze searched hers. "And no doubt what I reckon you're thinkin'."

Olive shifted against the stack of pillows, tucked a strand of hair behind her ear, and offered him the only thing at her disposal.

Gratitude.

"I appreciate everything you've done, Constable."

Jack smiled and settled his wide-brimmed hat back on his

head. He patted Roman's sturdy back and waved to the kids before exiting the way he'd come.

For the rest of the day, she insisted the kids stay inside. Close by her side.

Around dinnertime, Kate dropped by, and Miss Marie said her goodbyes.

For days now, it had been a quiet rotation—a revolving door of familiar faces taking turns on unofficial shifts to keep an eye on her.

She didn't ask for it.

Didn't quite know what to do with it, either.

After Jack's sister made dinner and helped with the kids' evening routine, Olive gathered Simon and Holly in the living room.

They curled up on either side of her as she read from the book they'd picked out.

That evening, she let them linger a little longer—soaking in the scent of baby shampoo and soap, the warmth of their small bodies pressed close.

She must've dozed off while Kate tucked them into bed and tidied the kitchen.

Sometime later, she stirred to a room cast in shadow, lit only by the soft glow of table lamps and the quiet twinkle of white lights beneath the cabinetry.

"Can I get you anything?" Kate asked, starting to rise. The springs in the easy chair gave a soft squeak.

Olive shook her head and asked the question on her mind.

"Can I assume there's a master schedule out there to keep tabs on me?"

Kate giggled. "Guilty as charged." She brushed at her blouse, then smoothed her hands down her pressed slacks.

"It was a collective effort." She winked.

But Olive wouldn't have been surprised to learn Hank was behind it.

"Oh! You may be interested to hear the Cartwright fellow tried to get away with a bad contract."

Seriously?

Olive's pulse tripled. "But they represent a multimillion-dollar corporation—"

The details didn't matter, did they?

Hank still owned the ranch.

Kate shrugged. "I don't have all the facts, yet—but the newspaper's publishing an exposé. To keep small business owners in the know."

Unbelievable. Hank had to be relieved beyond words.

All things are possible...

Indeed.

That included an expectant mom and her two- and four-legged kids falling in love with the town mechanic.

Baby Hart kicked. Olive rubbed the taut skin of her belly.

The idea should've scared her.

Instead, it only fueled her need to face Hank—and to assure him he wasn't to blame for going off the road with her kids.

To forgive him for his hurtful words.

And maybe—one day—they might even find their way back to a partnership in the garage. Or something more...

She didn't dare get ahead of herself. There were more pressing matters.

Hank was pulling an overnighter, but Mrs. S. had agreed to take the night shift.

I just need a small window of opportunity, Lord.

The next morning, a divine hiccup proved the answer to her prayer.

Mrs. Spagnoletti served up a delicious pancake breakfast. Afterward, a young church family picked up the kids and Roman for an outing to Sweetwater Lake.

It was when Pastor Mark's wife checked in to say she'd be running late.

With a twinge of guilt, knowing what she planned to do, Olive assured Mrs. S. she'd manage.

Once alone, she freshened up and changed into a loose-fitting sundress.

She grimaced at her reflection in the bathroom mirror. Purple smudges underscored too many restless nights.

She gathered her damp hair and pulled it into a ponytail.

Hank had seen her in far worse condition.

She stepped into the embroidered cowgirl boots Annie had packed after her ER visit, then flipped off the bathroom light.

Back in the kitchen, she grabbed her car keys and purse.

Granddad's Bible teetered on the edge of the oval table, open to Paul's letter to the Galatians. Her gaze caught on a yellow-highlighted passage.

She hesitated. How much time did she have before the pastor's wife showed up?

Curiosity won out. She picked up the Bible and skimmed the verse.

When she reached the final phrase, her heart hitched.

...but faith which worketh by love.

Until that moment, she hadn't realized there'd never been a day she wasn't trying to earn her way—with those around her. With God. The verse settled deep in her heart—He never asked for more than love.

Love for her neighbor. Love for herself.

It confirmed what she already knew. She was meant to begin with Hank.

Straightening her shoulders, she took a fresh breath.

Keys in hand, she breezed through the garage into a spring day promising a cloudless sky and golden sunshine. She soaked in the loamy richness of the earth, the citrus scents on the breeze. She even caught the faint whisper of the farm animals that once grazed the property.

Her gaze shifted to the edge of the gravel drive where her SUV was parked. She walked toward it, taking a few deliberate steps before managing to maneuver behind the wheel.

"Oh, goodness," she huffed, buckling in. She cranked the engine. Shifted into Reverse.

Depressed the gas pedal—

An invisible vice gripped her midsection. She gasped. Her foot slipped from the pedal.

Breathe.

The contraction was short-lived. A reminder that her window of opportunity was shrinking.

Her need to speak to Hank—to reassure him—hinted at a breakthrough.

She had nothing to prove.

But everything to gain.

When the pain subsided, she swallowed hard.

"Let's try this again."

She managed a clumsy three-point turn before a second contraction hit.

Liquid warmth pooled beneath her.

"Oh, dear."

It appeared God's plans differed from hers.

An engine hum pierced her subconscious. Tires crunched across gravel.

The tow truck's grille appeared head-on as it lurched to a stop. Hank's door flung open, and he hit the ground running.

A third contraction clamped down. Hard.

"Olive!"

Face inches from her driver's side window, she read the alarm in his eyes. She fumbled for the lock.

Without wasting a second, he hauled her into his arms and carried her to the truck. He gently settled her on the passenger seat and buckled her in.

The call to Sweetwater General was brief. His grip was steady, his fingers threaded through hers.

She barely remembered the drive to the ER or the swift delivery.

Emerson had arrived just in time to assist her OB. Guiding

Olive through the familiar steps, her expression was a mix of joy and grief. Her own inability to conceive was written plain across her face.

It was Baby Hart's first cries that grounded them both.

A flurry of activity welcomed her new daughter. Holly and Simon smothered their little sister with sloppy kisses.

Soon after, the town's vet led the kids from the private room—leaving Olive alone with the baby.

A knock at the door rattled her calm.

She ran her fingers through her hair, brushing against the plush lilac robe her friends had dropped off.

Pressing her lips to her daughter's downy head, she cleared her throat. "Come in."

The largest teddy bear she'd ever seen filled the doorway. Rivaled only by Hank himself.

The mechanic peeked around the stuffed toy and edged into the room.

His gaze drifted to the baby nestled beside her.

"Hey, there," he said, his voice thick with awe. A hitch in his breath. "She's beautiful—just like her momma."

Heat blossomed across Olive's cheeks. She dropped her gaze to Ivy Joy.

"Do you want to hold her?" She peeked up at Hank through damp lashes and caught the flicker of fear in his eyes.

Her daughter cooed. Pursed her perfect, rosy lips.

Olive watched the kaleidoscope of emotions move across Hank's face—the clench of his jaw. The slow easing of his shoulders.

He stepped forward, arms out, and tucked the baby against him like a football.

Ivy squirmed, then settled into the big man's arms.

Olive couldn't look away. "Hank."

His gaze snapped to hers—his expression unreadable.

"I don't blame you for the accident."

Hank took a steadying breath, eyes fixed on her. "I knew you wouldn't, and… Olive, I need to be honest. The reason I showed up at the ranch this morning…" He smiled, a little sheepishly. "You've had my heart since I caught you in my arms—the first of many times."

He chuckled, the sound a balm to her spirit.

She gulped. A tear slid down her cheek.

"And the only liability," he said, "is the risk of losing you."

Her heart squeezed. "What are you trying to say, Hank?"

A tiny cry from his arms interrupted the moment. He gently passed the baby back to her, then grasped his beard.

"What would you say about a permanent partnership—" He paused, raking a hand through his copper hair. "On and off the garage floor?"

Butterfly wings fluttered inside her. Hank's words, the eagerness in his gaze—so much like her son's.

Then he added, quiet but certain, "Olive… I love you."

Which made what she had to say all the harder.

Yes, she loved him. But the timing was wrong.

And the last thing she wanted was for Hank to feel jilted.

"The kids and I care for you so much, Hank…"

Unease crept into his eyes. "I'm sensing a 'but.'"

He wasn't wrong. Her family had fallen hard for the mechanic. But neither of them was ready for forever. Not yet.

"We both have issues to work through. To let God heal what's still broken."

Her voice wobbled, but she pushed on. "But I do love you, Hank. And I want to try—for the kids, for the future."

Relief softened the hard set of his jaw. His hand closed over hers, warm and steady.

"That's all I need," he said.

A yawn slipped out. She tried to fight the fatigue—

But not before she imagined his lips pressed to her forehead.

Instead of goodbye, it felt like a beginning.

Hank kept one eye trained on the Adirondack chair and two of the three females who'd stolen his heart.

Ivy Joy had made her surprise entrance into the world three weeks ahead of schedule.

And just that afternoon, both mother and newborn received a clean bill of health at their follow-up appointment.

Now the center of attention, Olive and Ivy were surrounded by a small circle of friends and church family in Kate's backyard.

Hank split the rest of his attention between Holly and Simon.

"Push us higher, Mr. Big!"

Holly pumped her legs. In front of the swing set, Josie, Finn, and Anthony waited for their turns—clapping and squealing.

Eighteen days had passed—not that he'd kept track—since moving the Harts into the single-level gingerbread cottage on Main Street. The home that once belonged to Jack and his late wife.

For the small get-together, Hank had slapped together his infamous surprise sandwiches—a special treat he used to make for Rosie, once upon a time.

Just a simple sandwich, really—two thick slabs of Annie's homemade potato bread, cut in quarters and packed with different fillings: peanut butter, raspberry preserves, slices of cheese, even leftover meatloaf.

He waited for the familiar punch of remorse to follow the memory.

Instead, warmth washed over him at the kids' reactions.

He chuckled, remembering their wide-eyed delight and giggles with each bite.

Olive waved at him.

His heart flipped in place.

He was used to it by now—ever since he'd quit fighting this thing between them.

"What can I whip up for ya, Big Country?"

Jack approached with a spatula in hand, his Stetson pushed off his forehead.

His sister had organized the little party to celebrate Baby Hart.

Truth be told, all Hank could think about was the next steps with Olive. They'd finally admitted their love, and being with her felt as natural as breathing. Or fishing. But asking for more hadn't felt right—yet.

At least Jack had managed to pin the rep from Cartwright with a contract technicality, which meant Hank's silence couldn't be twisted into an agreement—and any supposed transaction was now invalid.

The Harts' Lab came charging at him, and Hank grinned. "Surprise me."

Jack dodged the big dog and laughed. "You got it."

Hank reached down and scratched Roman between the ears. Took a deep breath, scented with lavender, fresh-cut grass, and meat grilling on the patio.

He turned back to the kids, watching as Holly and Simon sailed through the air, hands clasped, laughter trailing behind them as they raced over to grab Roman's leash.

They took off across the yard with their friends.

His attention drifted, easy as a breeze, back to Olive.

She crossed the lawn with her gaze locked on him.

Heat spread along his neck.

She wore her hair loose this afternoon, rippling over sun-kissed shoulders.

A flashback filtered in—his trip to the ranch a little more than three weeks ago, her car blocking the driveway.

His heart in his hand.

He'd muddled through a whole script on the drive. To ask for forgiveness.

To fight for her. For them.

But the sight of her car rocked him with doubt—fueled by a runaway fiancée.

Visions of Rosie's broken body had blocked everything else, forcing him into rescue mode.

Once at Sweetwater General, orderlies had whisked Olive into labor and delivery. He'd paced and asked himself the question he'd been avoiding the entire drive to the hospital.

Had she been running away?

Then Emerson appeared in the waiting room with Holly and Simon tucked against her. A sleepy smile lit up her face.

His chest had finally loosened.

"Mother and daughter are perfect," she'd said.

He'd exhaled a deep breath. Let go of his drive to fix everything and everyone.

And chose instead to trust God. Full stop—no matter what.

He was tired of holding on to guilt and grief.

What he wanted now was the peace Jesus promised. The kind that comes with surrender.

And here they were.

Surrounded by the love of chosen family and friends. It had taken hard work to get here—especially after Olive had gently postponed him with quiet, steady words at her hospital bedside.

He could eventually see God's hand in it all, using every setback in Hank's life to bring them together.

She had not been running away from him—as he'd once feared—but toward him.

"Hey, you."

She flashed him her secret smile reserved just for him, and it nearly curled his whiskers.

His gaze snapped to her empty arms.

She giggled and tipped his chin up with the brush of her finger, stealing his breath.

"Ivy Joy's making the rounds."

She leaned in for a quick hug, her floral fragrance lingering long afterward.

Schoolboy nerves took his tongue hostage. He still couldn't quite believe her interest in someone this side of forty. Grizzled around the edges, but slowly softening.

He raised the empty bottle of the inn's proprietary H_2O.

"Can I get you something to drink?"

"I thought you'd never ask." She winked, the gold flecks in her gaze swimming with mirth and affection.

Over the past few weeks, they'd both agreed there was truth to the town legend—that there really *was* "something in the sweet water." An uncontested fact across High Country—backed by Lacey's fervent prayers.

She fell in step beside him, fingers interlacing with his. As always, awareness zinged across his skin.

A comfortable silence wrapped them in a bubble as they approached a folding table waiting on the pavers.

She tilted her head back to meet his eyes. "How're the renovations coming along?"

Ah, yes—refurbishing the old barn.

After he'd helped the Harts move into Kate's cottage, he'd split his time between the garage and his ranch.

Olive's persistence had paid off.

Not to mention Annie's Cupcakes for a Cause fundraiser, the proceeds of which were being used to transform the barn into an event venue.

One that might even land in the Southwest's top wedding magazines.

Holly had dubbed it The Barn.

His new goal? Convince a certain new momma to be its first client.

Her slender fingers squeezed his, snapping him back to the present.

"Hank?" Her brow furrowed.

"Huh? Oh—right."

Reluctantly, he dropped her hand, grabbed a ladle, and poured iced water into a plastic cup.

"Annie just told me The Barn should be ready to hold events at the start of the year."

She'd also hinted at a trial run that fall. A Thanksgiving to remember.

He and Gordie had hired several new mechanics through The Lodge's apprenticeship program.

And until Olive returned as his right-hand person—something

they'd both been praying about—Gordie agreed to keep managing the college's interns.

"How wonderful!" Her eyes sparkled, rivaling the patio's twinkle lights. She sipped from the cup he handed her.

He took in her floral tank top and the flouncy skirt skimming her knees—and his went weak.

Once again, he thanked God for blessing him with this woman.

"—and I've got childcare set up for next weekend so I can teach our spring preventive maintenance class."

"Hi, guys!" Pastor Mark stepped up to the table, his thinning silver hair a testament to decades of shepherding the congregation.

After Olive was discharged from the hospital, they started individual counseling and were making steady progress.

They'd agreed their relationship would be built on a firm foundation of faith and nothing less.

"Thank you and your wife for coming tonight, Pastor."

She peeked around him. "Speaking of—where's your lovely bride?"

Mark laughed, the skin around his eyes crinkling. "I left her and the other ladies fussing over the newest member of our congregation."

Olive's whole face lit up. "Ivy has that effect on me, too."

"Especially since my wife claims credit for Baby Hart's early arrival." Pastor Mark chuckled—squeezed Hank's shoulder.

"Can I plan to see you both this week?"

They nodded.

Hank could only hope they'd be upgrading their sessions to *premarital* counseling.

"—don't you think?"

Olive cleared her throat.

Hank dropped his gaze to meet hers.

Lost in thoughts about the future, he hadn't realized they'd wandered into the side yard.

Overhead, a darkening sky revealed a smattering of stars that would soon pierce the shadows.

They stopped near a lavender bush, its sweet fragrance mingling with Olive's perfume.

She raised a brow, curiosity pooling in her gaze.

His heart swelled with affection. And more.

He swallowed. "What's that?"

A frown tugged at her glossy lips. "You seem preoccupied—did something happen at the garage?"

He coughed into his sleeve. Plucked the cup from her hand and set it on the lawn. His hands shook slightly as he clasped hers.

A breeze lifted a curl off her neck.

It was time to reel her in.

"Everything's fine, Olive." He clenched his jaw. Loosened it. Read the emotions in her golden eyes. Dared to believe they were both ready for more.

"You already know I've fallen for you, hook, line, and sinker—"

She giggled on a hiccup, unshed tears glistening on her lashes.

"And I'm ready to take our partnership to the next level. To be a family."

He paused, overwhelmed with love for this woman.

"And fill the ranch with laughter and love and more babies and—"

He heard the hitch in her breath.

Just before a shadow morphed into Roman as he barreled around the corner.

A sharp bark rang out.

His leash wrapped around their legs. Olive tumbled into him.

He caught her. Pulled her close.

And they burst into laughter.

She caught her breath, snuggled into his arms, and looked up at him.

"Oh, Hank, the five of us adore you."

His heart split wide open. Healed and whole.

Everything else faded—the guests, the lights, even the goofy dog sitting at their feet.

"Olive Catherine Hart—"

He'd rehearsed his speech all day. But somehow, it had sounded better in his head. He licked his lips. "Would you honor me by becoming my Valentine?"

She giggled again.

His pulse skyrocketed.

"Don't you think you're about three months late—"

And then her eyes widened as understanding bloomed. Roman woofed.

Hank did a double-take. If he didn't know better, he'd say he'd finally worked his way out of the doghouse.

"Roman!"

Holly and Simon clambered around the hedge—then skidded to a halt.

"There you are!" The kids stared at the grown-ups tangled together, Roman's leash still holding them hostage.

Unhurried, Olive pulled free. They helped untangle the Lab.

Then Olive turned to Holly and Simon, crouching to eye level. "So how do you guys feel about moving back to Mr. Big's ranch—as a family?"

Both children gasped—then launched themselves into Olive's arms.

Holly peeked up at Hank. "Does that mean I get to call you Daddy?"

He didn't believe his heart could expand any more. Thought Olive's words of love had been the best thing he'd ever heard. Until now.

He blinked back happy tears. "Do fish swim?"

All three of the Harts laughed, Roman adding two sharp barks.

Olive straightened—then drew Hank into their embrace.

He wrapped an arm around them and gazed into her eyes. "So…how do you feel about throwing a Thanksgiving wedding at The Barn?"

He didn't have to search hard to know she was about to make him the happiest man in all of High Country.

Starshine exposed the creamy expanse of her neck as she tilted her head and pressed her palms against his face.

"Do fish swim?"

His rib cage swelled—threatened to tear the seams in his shirt.

"Come on, Simon—" Holly tugged on her brother's hand "—I wanna tell Josie that Mr. Big's gonna be our new daddy!"

Simon grabbed Roman's leash, and they disappeared the way they'd come. Faint sounds drifted in from the side yard—signs the party was winding down.

He still had one more thing to do.

As soft as a whisper, he claimed Olive's lips. The sigh that shuddered through her lingered between them, warm and alive.

She pulled back just enough to look into his eyes, hers glowing. "You sure you're up for the job?"

Her breath tickled his whiskers, shooting tingles clear to his toes. But he also heard the fear behind her words, rooted in a lifetime of believing she was a burden.

He couldn't think of anything better than spending the rest of his days proving otherwise.

Arching his back, he puffed out his chest. "They don't call me Big Country for nothin'."

That's when Roman rocketed around the corner a second time—his leash trailing behind.

This time, Hank didn't think twice before hauling Olive into his arms and placing a gentle, fleeting kiss on her mouth.

Epilogue

Thanksgiving: six months later.

Even with her eyes trained on it, Olive could hardly believe the view.

She'd returned to The Barn after Ivy Joy's diaper change—the baby whisked from her arms by Lacey—and, not for the first time, did a double-take.

Gone were the scuffed floorboards, cobwebs, sagging roof, and rusted farm equipment, replaced by Holly's make-believe castle—complete with open-beam rafters and wide double doors opening to rolling pastures dappled by starlight.

And Olive had stepped into the role of a princess. But not the kind from storybooks and movies—a princess of the King.

A recent counseling session with Pastor Mark brought a Scripture to mind. One that spoke of her place in the Kingdom—an epiphany that confirmed her worth in Christ.

And helped her trust Hank's love. Whole and true.

She smoothed her hand down the pale yellow gown she found tucked among vintage apparel at Twice-Loved Treasures—paired with her blue-stitched cowgirl boots.

A nod to "something old…something blue," with Granddad's Bible the "something borrowed."

During the wedding march hours earlier, she'd taken slow, shallow steps across a rolled-out ruby carpet toward a trellis adorned in sprays of blooms from Sweetwater Floral—baby nestled against her side.

Her groom's idea of "something new."

Now her husband, the man shouldered his way across the dance floor where couples swayed to a ballad strummed by the town's "cowboy poet."

Gordie's wedding gift to them.

As the garage's silent partner, he'd also become a father figure to her—and a surrogate grandpa to the kids.

She'd asked him to give her away and still remembered their talk in the garage, his hand brushing away tears, and then his steady support as they walked down the aisle behind the wedding party.

Jack and Emerson. Annie and Josh. Lacey and Persh.

Even Eileen—Hope House's director—who'd helped bring her to Sweetwater.

She'd stood beside Kate, who Olive prayed might be next to find love.

Holly and Simon had served as flower girl and ring bearer—with Roman as, well… Roman.

As Hank reached her, she giggled at the memory of the black Lab in a white bow tie.

He lowered his head, his freshly trimmed whiskers brushing her neck. The butterflies stirred.

Pulling her close, he dropped his voice. "May I have this dance, Mrs. Valentine?"

His steady blue gaze met hers.

She exhaled a happy sigh. "Yes, you may, Mr. Valentine."

His hand, strong and sure, settled on her hip. The other clasped her fingers as he whisked her into the center of the room.

A laugh bubbled from her lips. He pulled her tighter. His chin grazed the waves Kate had arranged over her bare shoulders.

Within the safety of his arms, a new memory surfaced.

She'd been six or seven. Her mother had dropped her at Granddad's—then vanished again.

In his living room that afternoon, she'd stood before an old box radio as he turned a dial.

A tinny melody floated out. Granddad picked her up, set her feet on his, and danced across the wood floor until dusk.

"If The Barn's first event is any sign—you've done it again, Olive."

The recollection faded at Hank's words, but her heart stayed full.

Especially now.

Granddad's faith. His skills. His love.

All part of her. All part of this.

She grinned at Hank.

"You forgot the brilliant wedding gift you gave me."

Her chest swelled. He'd left no detail undone.

Hank nuzzled her neck. She leaned into him.

"Converting my old apartment into a nursery was a no-brainer."

"Sure," she drawled, pulling her hand from his chest to smack his shoulder. "I have a strong suspicion you had an ulterior motive."

Thanks to the baby monitor and nanny cam, she and Ivy had spent more time in Olive's happy place.

And Hank could keep an eye on them both.

"Happy Thanksgiving wedding day!"

The Pershings caught up with them as they left the dance floor—two-year-old Ada Mae perched on her daddy's shoulders.

Persh nodded his head at their daughter. She rubbed her eyes with a tiny fist.

"We're calling it a night. Someone's fading fast."

Olive glanced at Lacey, who stifled a yawn.

Her intuition told her it wasn't just Ada Mae. She suspected their little family would grow again soon. A secret smile tilted her lips as she hugged her friend.

She scanned the dance floor—the tables pushed aside after the holiday feast Annie's team catered.

She spotted Annie and Josh with Finn on his father's hip and newborn Ruby against Annie's chest.

They chatted with Emerson and Jack. The vet's copper-toned dress glowed beneath the lights.

Josie and Anthony lingered nearby—fawning over their family's recent blessing.

Hank clapped Persh on the back.

"Thank you, guys—for everything."

Olive smiled. "Truly."

Persh let out a hearty guffaw. Hitched a thumb at Lacey. "It was all Red's—er—my bride's doing."

She brushed his arm with a playful swat, then tugged on his lapel. "See you Sunday," she said, leading her husband away.

Hank dropped his hand from Olive's hip and nodded toward Holly and Simon. "Looks like I'm needed."

The kids waved from the refreshment table. He headed over.

Alone again, Olive's gaze drifted to Emerson, who stood beside Josie and Anthony with a baby nestled in her arms.

God had fulfilled her dream that summer—through the firehouse's first Safe Haven drop-off.

Within weeks, the child had been placed with the Wellses—adding to their family in a way that had once seemed impossible.

Olive blinked back tears. Their baby hadn't been Sweetwater's last adoption.

You're truly the God who sees us.

Her whispered prayer—once spoken in desperation—rose again in gratitude.

She spotted her family. Every kind of goodie circled a glass punch bowl of the inn's proprietary sweet water, while Hank balanced a stack of dessert plates piled high, the two kids who officially called him Dad flanking him with bright, eager eyes.

They returned to her just as Hank's phone buzzed in his tuxedo pocket.

Tows were less common now, thanks to the new quarterly preventive maintenance classes. But they still happened.

And plans were in place for a second truck once The Barn's bottom line allowed.

As Hank pulled out his phone, Olive searched his eyes.

"Want to sneak out and take the run together?" She knew her kids would find a ride home. That was the Sweetwater way.

"Nah." A mischievous spark lit his eyes. He kissed her nose, then pulled some keys from his jacket.

They sailed through the air—caught by Angel.

The teen, now a skilled protégé on his way to becoming a master mechanic, raised his brows. "Boss?"

Her chest swelled with pride at how much her husband had grown—learning to let go, to release his need to be Mr. Fixit for everybody, and to recognize that he was just as worthy of love as anyone.

She'd grown, too—learning to release old lies and rest in the truth that she was loved, seen, and cherished by the God who had answered a mother's prayer in ways she'd never expected.

"Go ahead, son. As you can see, I'm tied up with my new bride."

He leaned in, trailing his lips over Olive's.

She laughed. "Watch it—Roman hasn't tripped us with his leash...yet."

Hank waggled his eyebrows, a smirk tugging at his mouth. "Since when do I need an excuse?"

Then he pulled her into his strong arms.

Right where she'd always belonged.

* * * * *

Olive's Strawberry Feta Spinach Salad Recipe

Salad Ingredients *Servings: 12*

2 pints of fresh strawberries
½ cup slivered or sliced almonds, toasted
10 ounces fresh spinach
½ cup crumbled feta cheese
⅔ cup homemade strawberry balsamic vinaigrette

Vinaigrette Ingredients *Servings: 16*

⅔ cup roughly chopped strawberries
3 tablespoons apple cider vinegar
2 tablespoons honey, or agave
2 tablespoons fresh lime juice
1 teaspoon lime zest—about 1 large lime
½ teaspoon salt
⅓ cup olive oil

Vinaigrette Instructions

Place the strawberries, vinegar, honey (or agave), lime juice, lime zest, and salt in a small food processor and process until the strawberries are broken down. Stop and scrape sides often. Once mixed, with the food processor running, stream in olive oil until dressing is mixed and thickened.

Salad Instructions

Rinse, pat dry, and slice strawberries. Set to the side. Heat a frying pan on high heat, add the sliced almonds, and continuously mix for 30–60 seconds until golden brown. Be careful not to burn. In a large salad bowl, add the fresh spinach, ¾ of the strawberries, half the crumbled feta, and half the sliced almonds. Pour in a small amount of vinaigrette and toss the salad until coated; add more if needed. Top with remaining strawberries, toasted almonds, and crumbled feta. Enjoy immediately, or refrigerate up to 2 hours before serving.

Salad recipe source: katiescucina.com
Vinaigrette recipe source: onehotoven.com
Any modifications are mine.

Dear Reader,

I hope you enjoyed your return trip to Sweetwater—where a town legend, meddling matchmakers, and divine interruptions are part of every journey.

Like Hank and Olive, you may have known what it means to feel broken or unseen. But God hears. He sees. He heals. And He delights in redeeming our stories through Jesus, which often includes detours and helping hands along the way.

My prayer is that this story brings you hope, laughter, and a reminder that happy endings of the heart—God's kind—are always possible.

Because of readers like you, Sweetwater just might grow again. Stay tuned! Until then, I'd love to stay in touch—visit me at chrismadayschmidt.com and sign up for my newsletter.

Always,
Chris

Get up to 4 Free Books!

We'll send you 2 free books from each series you try
PLUS a free Mystery Gift.

Both the **Love Inspired®** and **Love Inspired® Suspense** series feature compelling novels filled with inspirational romance, faith, forgiveness and hope.

YES! Please send me 2 FREE novels from the Love Inspired or Love Inspired Suspense series and my FREE gift (gift is worth about $10 retail). I may cancel anytime by emailing ReaderServiceInfo@Harlequin.com or by calling 1-800-873-8635. If I don't cancel, I will receive 6 brand-new Love Inspired Larger-Print books or Love Inspired Suspense Larger-Print books every month and be billed just $7.19 each in the U.S. or $7.99 each in Canada. That is a savings of 20% off the cover price. It's quite a bargain! Shipping and handling is just 75¢ per book in the U.S. and $1.75 per book in Canada.* I understand that accepting the free books and gift places me under no obligation to buy anything—they are mine to keep for free no matter what I decide.

Choose one: ☐ **Love Inspired Larger-Print** (122/322 BPA G3CD)   ☐ **Love Inspired Suspense Larger-Print** (107/307 BPA G3CD)   ☐ **Or Try Both!** (122/322 & 107/307 BPA G3CE)

Name (please print)

Address   Apt. #

City   State/Province   Zip/Postal Code

Email: Please check this box ☐ if you would like to receive newsletters and promotional emails from Harlequin Enterprises ULC and its affiliates. You can unsubscribe anytime.

> **Mail to the Harlequin Reader Service:**
> **IN U.S.A.:** P.O. Box 1341, Buffalo, NY 14240-8531
> **IN CANADA:** P.O. Box 603, Fort Erie, Ontario L2A 5X3

Want to explore our other series or interested in ebooks! Visit **www.ReaderService.com** or call **1-800-873-8635.**